SECOND BOOK OF THE SPACE TRILOGY

TALES FROM GRANDAD

TRAVEL ABOVE
THE SPEED OF LIGHT

DON KEIRLE

CHAPTER 1

CAN THIS REALLY BE DONE?

Every one knew that travel above the speed of light was impossible until Captain Johnson and the Prof actually did it. No one knows as yet how they achieved it but researchers are examining the flight recorders of the Solar Orbiter in minute detail, to check on conditions. So far this has not yielded a result.

The senior technicians involved approached the director of space research a certain Helen Svensson, and asked if an approach could be made to the Prof before he became too old to be of service. Helen had immediately distinguished herself as a research assistant to the Whistler, and he was still her boss but she had flowered to such a degree that he allowed her total freedom to chase whatever moonbeams came her way. In this instance she deferred to him. He was minded to visit the Prof as a friend more than anything else, so a date was agreed.

The Prof met them with a large smile and said "Well you pair took your time!"

He ushered them into his living room which gave an open view of his garden. This was festooned with plants of numerous exotic varieties but pride of place went to his beloved runner beans.

The Prof was still as mentally active as ever, and asked them how they were getting on in their research into faster than light travel.

"Not too brilliantly" replied the Whistler. "We have gone over and over the flight data and there is absolutely no clue as to how you did it!"

The Prof sat down and said, "Well I wondered about that myself. When I think of the gravity motor and how it responds to the warp web out in space another idea suddenly struck me, though I have no scientific basis for the notion!"

"Go on" urged Helen.

"Well I do not think that Einstein was wrong, just not quite complete; I just think that somewhere there could be points in space that are somehow absolutely neutral, and if you use rocket power while you are in them, then the ship will accelerate, and thus you may be able to penetrate them, and somehow end up going faster than light. Now if that is true then we were as close to being lost in space as it was possible to get, because we would have had to have chanced on two such areas to penetrate in and extract ourselves back."

Helen noticed that the Whistler had gone quiet, and that his face had assumed the robot like calm as it always did while he was lost in thought. It was as though all of his energy was taken up in thought; leaving none for generation of facial expression.

Silence pervaded the room as the Prof smiled across to Helen saying "he always goes like this when he is on to something!"

Helen already knew this from her own association with him but her reaction startled the Prof.

"Please don't ask my husband to be the guinea pig!"

"You're still married to Henrik then?" enquired the Prof.

"Of course I am! We are expecting our firstborn in about seven months" smiled Helen.

"Ah!" sighed the Prof, "I understand your little outburst now."

The Whistler suddenly resurfaced, "Yeeesss!!! It wasn't just what you did, it was also where you were, and your vector direction when you did it! You went through a black tunnel. I just thought of that name to describe a sort of gateway to the other side."

He went silent again, then resurfaced fully. "I think a volunteer crew will be required to check things out and we could use one of the shuttles, because we will need to be close to the speed of light when we make the attempt. First though I will check on the gravity web points and try to see how many neutrals there are, and try to reason out exactly how you got back. Come on Prof, break out the whisky, we've got work to do aplenty!"

"You will use only crew members that have no family won't you?" said Helen with some anxiety.

The Whistler stared at her and then relaxed into a genuine smile of pleasure "you are expecting!" he chuckled.

"True" she said, "though I admit I haven't even seen a doctor yet."

"Prof, I know you are retired but I will issue you with a personal pass to any world space centre so if you have any more bright ideas you can get them across to me. You know with the holographic televisions now you could be any where in the world but I could see you as if you were standing right with me. There's a centre only about twenty miles from here so I will send you a good old e-mail if I feel the need to chat, and it wouldn't take you away from your beloved garden!"

The Prof knew he hadn't heard the last of this yet and felt a strange satisfaction that he could still be of use, and suddenly felt a kinship with the old archivist known only as Grandad.

Two hours after his visitors had departed his computor beeped quietly and he had an e-mail from Catherine Whistler asking if she could bring her little brood along to see him.

The Prof was delighted and e-mailed back that she would be welcome literally at any time.

Three days later Catherine appeared at the door with her two children.

"I see you've got one of each now, Catherine "he smiled as he stood aside to welcome them in.

"Right-ho I've come for some scuttlebutt, I've seen the initial reports from James Whistler and now I want to hear the facts!"

"Well I was about to sit down for my Sunday lunch, would you like some?" he grinned.

"Well I couldn't very well come all this way and go without getting some of the legendary runner beans down me" she grinned in return.

Another of the Prof's qualities was that he wasn't a bad cook. Catherine almost drooled at the dinner he served up, a lovely, lip smacking Sunday roast.

Catherine's children sat in awed silence for most of the meal, but they soon fell under the spell of the shear charm of the Prof.

Catherine talked on only one real subject and that was Eric Whistler. "I hope they don't ask him to captain the experimental ship you know" she confided.

"That's both you and Helen Johnson, erm Svensson, think that" the Prof informed her.

"Ah, she must be preggers!" interpreted Catherine. The Prof raised a smiling eyebrow.

Mind you the fact that two women had expressed this sentiment gave the Prof an idea as the word safety popped into his mind.

CHAPTER 2

THE PROF'S IDEA

The Prof's idea was as always simple and basic, and he could think of no reason why it shouldn't be done. He went to the local offices of the space administration and used his new pass to gain entry, and then asked for help in setting up communications with James Whistler.

One of the junior operatives remembering his face from the mule trial saga rushed off to organise the necessary, muttering that they had the Prof on the premises. Mention of that and everyone in the building was keen to know what was going on, and took every opportunity to peep round corners and over screens at him. He had become the Robin Hood of his time.

The Prof was asked if he needed full security, and he said that this was a matter for James Whistler.

The Whistler soon came across the ether and exactly as he had said, the holographic TV transmission made it look as if he was standing in the room quite close by. The Prof marvelled at this because it was a recent development and had not yet reached the public domain.

"Hello Prof" the Whistler's voice rang out slightly hollowly, "what can we do for you today?"

"It's to do with your notion of an experimental run in space" he began "some folk have expressed an idea that started me thinking."

"Go on" encouraged the Whistler.

"Well it is as much to do with safety as costs, but it could improve the one and reduce the other in certain circumstances. The idea is that the experimental ship only be crewed until a short while before the experiment, then use an automatic system to go through the experiment much as we did when we sent old Trueblood back to earth."

He continued "if we send two ships on the mission the second ship can act as a lifeboat to the crew of the first ship. Thus when the experiment is under weigh, we would have a number of experienced space operatives close at hand, and they could report on anything unusual from their own perspective and should be able to give invaluable assistance. When the experimental ship has gone through its programme the crew could reboard and again tell if anything unusual had occurred!"

"Well Prof I must have caught a little bit of your mindset because we have organised to do exactly that though we plan to put a third ship a little further off just in case!"

"Brilliant! So you don't need me then," chuckled the Prof.

"May be, maybe not" smiled the Whistler, "but what I will do is to keep you in the loop once the experiment is ongoing, if you don't mind that is!"

"Very kind, and after all runner beans only have a limited charm you know!" spluttered the Prof who had just swallowed a mouthful of coffee the wrong way.

CHAPTER 3

SOME OF THE WHISTLER'S INVESTIGATIONS

James Whistler had a very deep thinking ability. He got Helen Johnson to construct a detailed computor controlled graph showing all of the significant gravity lines around the areas in space where the Solar Orbiter had made the leap. Helen endeavoured to make lines thicker where gravity was stronger and thinner where the opposite was true.

When Helen took her results to the Whistler, even he was surprised by the outcome.

The Prof's idea that there were gravity neutral points was valid but the Solar Orbiter had not made the leap at one of these points. The point of the leap was in an area bounded by neutral gravity points but the actual point of transition was where all gravity lines were in accord as if some exterior force was constraining or focussing the lines to follow a given direction.

More research showed that there were other similar geometric patterns occurring elsewhere but that there were not that many of them. They all had a three dimensional circular or elliptical boundary of gravity neutrals, but in the midst there was a concentration of gravity lines of immense density.

The Whistler knew that only he himself had sufficient blended experience of space travel and scientific ability to make the necessary deductions from the information now available, but he filtered out one area of study and asked Helen if she would plot these over the whole of the Solar system between the earth and the Saturnian system. He wanted this done on the basis that further space exploration would be unlikely to go to the inner planets.

Over the coming weeks, Helen succeeded in doing just that and there were a number of neutral groups and she decided to add and highlight them into galactic charts so that future space captains would know exactly where they may make the jump.

She presented her work to the Whistler and he set about examining each of the highlighted points in minute details. Once he had verified the application of certain mathematic principles he once again asked Helen for her help. Between them they engineered a pictorial representation of the fields inside the highlighted areas. There was a point in each one where the distortion of the web lines resembled a whirlpool and had an entrance hole clearly visible, but there were others that had more of a stalagmite appearance and stuck upwards, in a pattern that was reminiscent of the bottom of a twister, except that it had a pointed top.

Their best guess was that some were entrances and some were exits. This idea appeared to be sound, as the Solar Orbiter had gone through one type and come back through the other. The Whistler asked Helen to re-mark the charts so that the entrance black tunnels and the exit blue tunnels as they decided to call them were clearly differentiated.

"I wonder what the Prof would think of our latest theories," mused Helen.

"Until we have proved our theories with a mission, they will stay as theories but I've already e-mailed the Prof with our findings. Ok I think it is home time for us and I wouldn't be surprised if we have an e-mail from the Prof, tomorrow morning. See you then" said the Whistler as he doffed his hat at Helen and went speedily out of the lab door.

"He is up to something" thought Helen but she had no idea what it was.

The following morning the Whistler was absent from the lab, an almost unheard of precedent. Helen had thought deeply about the transition from normal time and space to whatever lay beyond. She decided that that there would be a requirement for a separate chart with all of the blue and black holes clearly marked. Now on the normal side she already had enough information to plot all of these within the earth to Saturn range, but she had no idea what was available on the "other side". She constructed a blank chart ready to plot all of the transition holes, with means to cross reference them as a galactic geographic link.

As understanding of the situation increased this second chart would prove to be redundant, but that was some way off yet.

She put herself metaphorically speaking on the "other side" and an idea occurred to her as she was imagining what exactly may be going on there. She realised that something had moved the Solar Orbiter, in such a way that she gained distance without losing time. Helen began to think of the other side as a new gravity web, and wondered if all of the web lines in normal space time had links through the transition holes, "portals", and looped back through another portal so that normal time had the web as we know it but the return path of each line went through on the other side. She decided that as people already called the normal bit "the ether" she would call the companion, "the rethe". If her idea was sound the rethe would provide a number of direct line links to other portals and a ship would be able to traverse them once it could establish on a given line. Her idea was also that the lines on the rethe were not in normal time space relationships, and that time was simply not there, so the jump would take no time at all.

The time element in the case of the Solar Orbiter had come from within the ship itself and comprised the total time taken to turn the ship round and begin the return to normal existence. Perhaps purely by chance the Solar Orbiter had found entrance and exit portals so that the course of the ship remained unaltered, but a large slice of time had simply been cut away. If this idea proved sound it would mean that any ship would simply maintain its course and would not get lost. She wondered if time travel would end up as a by product of these notions. Possibly, but she did not want to cloud her judgement with another branch of possibilities just now. What would have happened if the Solar Orbiter had remained on the other side for a longer period of time? Again her mind simply explored its own notions. If time spent on the other side was only there by a means which was proportioned by the real time activities of the spaceship crew, then was found to be inversely proportional to the real time in the ether it would mean that the longer the Solar Orbiter had spent on the other side, then the shorter the real time taken for the journey. Thus if it had spent a week there, then they would have cut more time from the ether journey than if they spent an hour or a second there. This idea was exciting and needed full discussion with the Whistler. It appeared that the time sliced off any journey would be still under the control of the spaceship commander. If by dint of certain circumstances some ship got into the rethe and then exited immediately back into the ether then there may be time added to rather than cut from the journey. This definitely had a smell of time travel about it!

The Whistler still hadn't shown up yet. Helen sent an e-mail to the Prof asking if she and the Whistler could visit to discuss progress. The Prof e-mailed straight back saying that the Whistler was expected at his place at any moment.

"Wait for me," she e-mailed straight back.

Some hours later she arrived at the Prof's place to find the two men earnestly discussing something. They both rose as she walked straight round into the back garden.

"Ok boys I've got something that needs somebody clever to tell me where I've gone wrong" she blurted out. "Computor, please!" she imperiously snapped her fingers sharply. The grinning Prof moved as quickly as he could to get his laptop. Helen put in her flash memory unit and opened her programme. The two men listened to her excited discourse and were blown away by the depths she had probed and the way her theory all knitted together so neatly.

"My God" expostulated the Whistler, "the same germ of an idea had occurred to me and I was just expounding it to the Prof, when you got here, but you have gone much, much farther than me. I think over the next few days we will try to discredit it in order to prove you wrong, but I must say that I will be astounded if you are shown to be wrong in any way.

Frankly I think that is the most incredible piece of research work that I have ever seen and you must be recognised for your efforts. You will be famous!"

Helen grinned. "I was almost afraid to tell you about it, because if I am wrong then I will be bitterly disappointed!"

"Well" chimed in the Prof, "you may be incorrect in some small detail, but I am sure that when you check out the figures for the time gained by the Solar Orbiter, it will fit your theory!"

She pinked very slightly and the Whistler beamed at her, "you have already done that haven't you?"

"Yes I have" she smiled, "and that is really why I wanted your opinion. After all that part of the enterprise is part of your remit, not mine, but I couldn't resist checking things out. It was only gut instinct that told me that when you weren't at work you would be here, and I was itching to tell you both about it."

"Yes I should have told you what I was doing Helen. It was very remiss of me not to. I did it for security reasons of course, and though I had had as I say, the germ of that idea I was just bouncing off the Prof to see if we could tear it down, and here you are with the whole idea just about cut and dried!"

"Can I tell Henrik about my idea? She asked.

"I think that you can, and I think that this point on space exploration, we are going to need the combined efforts of Johnson, Whistler, and Svensson, to crew the experimental mission ships. Why don't we have a party, held here at the Prof's place and we can all get here using normal transport so it shouldn't arouse any suspicion, in say a fortnights time?!"

Helen nodded and then said "You know, I was trying to reconcile the amount of time cut from the Solar Obiter's journey, and the time clocks readings on the ship itself and the idea of the inverse function struck me. I wrestled with it for a bit, arbitrarily decided to add a couple of constants in and then bingo when I put our only known source of information in, the answer came out pretty well spot on!"

Fast forward now and Captain and Jane Johnson were the first to arrive, complete with their brood. They had barely had time to say hello when a taxi drew up and disgorged Eric and Catherine Whistler and their children, and the Whistler.

Half an hour later a powerful motorcycle and sidecar arrived and as helmets were removed the Svensson's walked up the drive and knocked.

"Before proceeding any further please drink a toast to the space musketeers." Eric Whistler poured out his glasses of Martian elixir, and handed them all round the adults. "All for one and one for all!" As they sipped the wine unashamedly pinching the phrase straight from the famous Dumas novel. The kids were all playing hide and seek in the Prof's intricately planted garden, leaving the adults free to chat.

Catherine Whistler smiled at Helen and said "preggers?!" Helen glanced guiltily across to Henrik and with finger across lips said "Shhhh!"

"Sorry," grinned Catherine, but this time Henrik caught a whiff of something in the air.

"Sorry about what?" he enquired.

"She is sorry that she nearly blabbed out about who is pregnant!" said Helen.

"Ah!" smiled Henrik, "so who is pregnant?"

The room had all become aware of this little aside and everyone laughed.

Helen grinned and with a delicious expression on her face asked "Why are men so thick?"

Inside the mind of Henrik Svensson a penny ever so gently fell, and he looked up at the assemblage and said "perhaps I am thicker than most but you had better come here, wife!" as he opened his arms and his face was suffused with shear delight.

After dining with the cracking repast served up by the Prof and drinking more of Eric's Martian elixir, the party got down to business. The Whistler stood up and tapped the side of his glass with a knife. Silence fell.

"Ladies and gentlemen" he began, "I think it is fair to say that we have probably made a real breakthrough. As the most senior researcher in the world space institute it should be down to me to inform you of the news that we have, but in this instance I shall defer to the person who more than any other has pieced together the route by which we will be able to travel faster than light. I give you Helen Svensson! Come on Helen, get up, you are on!"

Helen got to her feet and glanced nervously around the room. All eyes were upon her and she cleared her throat.

"To use a phrase made popular by the Prof, I have chanced on a line of reasoning that seems to explain what the Solar Orbiter got up to! As you know almost all things have a go and return function. That is to say a sort of feedback whereupon every action has an equal and opposite reaction. In the real world we have time and dimensions and speed, and every type of motion was explained by Newton's laws. That is until a certain man by the name of Albert Einstein came on the scene. Newton's laws were not wrong just not complete and Einstein's ideas on relativity explained certain discrepancies that Newton's laws could not explain. Now it appears that perhaps Einstein's laws were not complete either, or rather that there is an existence not covered by Einstein's laws."

Helen went through her ideas from beginning to end and then paused for a moment to sip from her glass. As she was doing this there was a spontaneous applause which died the moment she looked up again. "I have used my ideas as a predictive test and using data gathered from the Solar Orbiter and found that they correlated almost exactly with the time you gained and your re-entry point into normal time zones. It would appear that your course once established does not vary when you are in the rethe, so long as there is a blue escape tunnel in line with your course. The longer it takes you to get into your blue escape tunnel, the shorter the real time journey becomes. Traversing from the ether to the rethe and back would appear to invert time."

She sat down and a hubbub of astounded comments burst out from the gathering.

Jane Johnson looked at her husband and could see the fatherly pride oozing from him. She smiled inwardly as she knew he was equally proud of his more recent family.

Captain Johnson spoke "so it looks like we three spaceman are being lined up for another space trip!" he was nodding while smiling.

"I am afraid you will have to be patient" slurped the Prof who really was getting a taste for the Martian elixir; strangely even though he was a shareholder he had not drunk it regularly. "The plan is to send three ships up but the shuttle that makes the jump will be uncrewed. You will be stationed as observers only and will reboard the shuttle when she re-appears. If she re-appears," he added warily. "If Helen's theory is correct the shuttle should re-appear about 200,000 thousand miles further on after about half an hour!"

Eric Whistler quietly smiled; he looked across at Captain Johnson and said "now you know what it feels like to be ordered to stay on the sidelines, Kingdom!"

Captain Johnson smiled ruefully and said "well at least we shouldn't have to worry about the mule!"

The rest of the evening went as most parties do with the men playing with the children and the women chatting about women things. Helen finally said "well this party is even sweller than the last one!"

The Prof offered them all a room for the night as at was far too late to be thinking of going home and anyway the flights wouldn't have been till the next day. In the morning the Prof found he had gained another title and this was "Grandad" donated to him by the children. He was quite pleased about this and asked Catherine what her grandad's name actually was.

Catherine's sense of humour surfaced as she quipped "it sure wasn't Bill Wild or Wild Bill for that matter!" adding more soberly "His wife had died years before so I only ever heard my mom and dad call him "Dad" and I always called him "Grandad". I think it may have been Ted, short for Edward. He had arranged all the details of his own funeral and so I didn't even get to look at his death certificate. Silly I know but I simply don't know his surname. I will find out and let you know."

The Prof chuckled as he heard his own name mentioned as he remembered childhood pals calling him Wild Bill after the cowboy of that name.

The Prof felt quite well in himself but he knew he was unlikely to see a hundred. Nevertheless he felt he would see the next phase of space adventure unfold, and he privately thought he would last into his nineties. It was comforting to think that he still had a possible fifteen years left.

CHAPTER 4

The mission gets under weigh

THE CREWS GET WELL REPAIRED

Captain Johnson as he preferred to be called although he now held the rank of Space Admiral took the full crew of each shuttle and gave them all a pre-prepared lecture on what had happened on the first jump. He made sure that every crewmember was word perfect and could bring each significant point of that journey to mind immediately. The day arrived and three shuttles each with provisions for three months on board ran along the ramp and were launched into space. They had an earth orbit rendezvous as the final checkpoint before departure, using rocket power to get to escape velocity then gravity motor controls for onwards into the ether. All this was now standard procedure for any earth launched venture and went exactly according to plan. On approach to the designated jump zone all three ships were at warp 0.95, and Henrik Svensson's ship had been rigged up with the auto control function. Henrik and his four crewmen set the auto procedure, timed to begin 5 minutes after they had left the ship. Each man used his personal propulsion pack to make the short journey across to Eric Whistler's vessel. Eric then began the evasive manoeuvre but found his ship was sluggish in response; nevertheless he reached his designated area and turned his ship to observe. As the uncrewed vessel began by switching off the gravity control, it seemed to jump a couple of feet then became visually distorted and vanished "down the plug hole" as Henrik Svensson put it.

"My blood has just run cold" Henrik confessed, and then they waited and after half an hour, then an hour there was still no sign of the vessel re-emerging anywhere. Eric requested and got a full meeting on board Captain Johnson's vessel. They discussed what had gone on. From Captain Johnson's viewpoint the uncrewed vessel simply vanished but the Whistler and Svensson crews agreed to a man that there had been a small jump followed by the plug-hole effect as it was to become known.

Henrik Svensson requested a look at the Whistler and Johnson computors, grunted and then got his own out and booted it up. "*There* is the problem he said pointing at the screen on his own computor. There was a small speck on it and it looked for all the world like a decimal point. It wasn't though, and he was big enough to admit that he hadn't noticed it before. Captain Johnson had managed to persuade his daughter to loan him a copy of her programme with regard to time and inverse time calculations. He plugged in the flash memory and began to load it in. Even with the best laptops available it was still going to take about 4 hours. "Ok boys, I know we haven't much room but before we disperse back to our two ships I suggest a good old game of cards. Eric Whistler was virtually unbeatable. He had been schooled in the mathematical probabilities by the Whistler and he was well enough educated to remember most of what he had been taught. A little bit of sly collaboration between Henrik and Captain Johnson did however manage to put one over on him after a while. Eric knew that some fiddling had been done and grinned widely when they informed him how they had teamed up against him. The computor beeped, the programme loading was complete.

Captain Johnson entered the parameters into Helen's programme and waited while it chewed the figures up and it finally spat out 1341 hours. "Crikey that's almost 8 weeks" ejaculated Henrik, "all due to one speck of dirt!"

"Aye, well it's cheaper to sit out here than go back to earth and come back, so await we must" said the mission leader resignedly.

Captain Johnson radioed back to earth and asked for the Whistler.

"James Whistler here," came the anxious enquiry.

"Triple mission commander here", intoned Captain Johnson. "We have a godsend opportunity to really test Helen's theory," he began, and he outlined what had gone on.

"Ok" murmured the Whistler "I will run the figures through the latest programme and see if it produces different results, in the meantime we have nothing to do but to wait. It was a good decision to provide you with supplies for three months it has saved additional journeys. By the way I promised the Prof I would keep him in the loop, so long as you don't mind!"

"If it were any one else I probably would mind but that old guy has something that none of the rest of us have, so please do so with my blessing, Johnson out."

Well seven weeks and six days later the two ships were stationed so that they would flypast the return point about 500 miles either side. And suddenly neither ship was fully responsive to controls so each man had his rocket motors on dribble fed just in case. Exactly as Helen had predicted the jump ship reappeared preceded by the reverse of the distortion seen on the way in. Henrik's crew re-boarded their ship and checked all systems out and found that the on board clocks had only moved by a few seconds from their departure time. Everything else seemed to be in full working order, so Captain Johnson gave the order to return to earth. This went exactly as one would have expected. Henrik's ship was quarantined for a full year while the Whistler's lab men went over it almost one atom at a time. No fault of any sort was found. Helen's work was published and suddenly she had the media on her tail almost 24 hours a day.

She mused that James Whistler had been crafty in letting her assume full credit whilst he who had played a sizeable part in proceedings remained as a back room boffin, and retained his notoriety in its smaller form.

Luckily she had other fish to fry and soon produced a noisy squawking healthy baby boy. She was staggered at the amount of attention a baby requires and finally slept through the night after about 6 weeks. She really wasn't sure if the baby had truly slept through or whether she had become so tired that she had slept through the baby's cries.

"It's the same for all parents" her dad told her, "but the result is the same, at least you get some rest."

A few weeks later Catherine Whistler and Jane Johnson arranged to come round to see how she was getting on. The boy looked more like Helen than Henrik but he had striking blond hair. There were no major developments from the space agencies and so family lives settled back to their normal activities. Helen knew that she would be in demand sooner or later and so employed a young girl nanny who had come over to earth for a holiday from mars. This girl was non other than Venus, and so being the first earthling born extra terrestrially some how seemed an appropriate person for the job. Her first few weeks were spent acclimatising to the greater gravity on earth and this she did but it took immense efforts of will before she was comfortable again.

CHAPTER 5

JAMES WHISTLER PUTS HIS THINKING CAP ON

The news of the latest tests somehow leaked out and the world was buzzing with the idea that one could actually travel faster than light. The Whistler was unhappy with this. He was a scientist of some note and had studied Einstein's theory of relativity deeply.

He was unhappy at appearing to break this law. The Solar Orbiter had been and done it, but how it had been achieved was still a partial mystery, though beams of dappled illumination were shining generally at the issue. Half of the worlds leading intellectuals thought the law couldn't be broken and thus the whole thing was an elaborate con trick, and of the rest some showed a flawed understanding of Einstein's law. There was only a handful of folk who's thought processes he felt he could trust and of these no-one had an explanation. This was a unique time. Einstein had been ahead of his time. He had produced a theory that took years of endeavour to prove, but in this case an action, a successful action had occurred ahead of any suitable theory.

He found Helen's young mind was still very open and discussed things with her over a protracted period. He himself felt that a key to understanding the whole thing lay with the as yet unexplained distortion visually observed just as the jumps to and from were made. He also felt that the effect on the manoeuvrability, of the space ships nearby was inextricably part of the puzzle.

Due to tests on earth with the Hadron Large Collider particle accelerator in Europe, the ability to accelerate a particle was known to have an end. When almost at the speed of light even an electron gained mass to such a degree that it would take infinite force to actually accelerate it to warp factor 1.0. Some subatomic particles had been recorded as travelling faster than light. Yet he knew that somehow a ship as large as the Solar Orbiter had unexpectedly got into the rethe.

"There must be an equal and opposite reaction to every action - except for the flywheel gyroscope" he thought. His mind raced ahead and he found himself running to Helen's office. He wanted to yell "eureka" but confined himself to English as he puffed "Helen I think I may have it!"

She smiled sweetly at him, and said "James there is that much air going in and out of you at this moment I can suddenly understand why you are known as the Whistler! Slow down draw breath and tell me. I am all ears."

He composed himself and began "for every action there is an equal and opposite reaction. I do not believe that we have *travelled* faster than light; it only seems as if we have. Imagine the use of old fashioned logarithms. In there, the function of multiplication is done more simply by addition but at each end of the process you have to jump into the log process and then use the anti-log to get back out. I think that the black tunnel leads into a world of anti-matter and that positive matter cannot exist there. I believe that there must be links between the two existences, and that inward black tunnels are equally balanced by outward blue tunnels so that the matter and anti-matter states can co-exist. If this were not the case then one would surely swallow the other and, well, who knows what that may entail, probably the creation of a black hole or a big bang. I further believe that as the ship makes the jump, a cloak of anti-matter is somehow generated to maintain the equal status, and during this generation the ship is partly in each domain simultaneously. This only stays evident for a few seconds, and accounts for the visual distortion seen. As soon as the ship is fully cloaked the jump in is completed.

The ship is then in the anti-matter domain. The anti matter domain has protected itself by cloaking the intruding positive matter, which fortunately protects the ship as well. Should we have two ships in there together I suspect that transfer between them would be nigh impossible because each cocoon is exactly that, there is no easy way out of it.

Now in this world of anti matter we have no time element. But when you exit it, we find that ether time has been inverted. The apparent time in the anti-matter domain is the reciprocal of time in our domain exactly as you predicted with your notion.

The lucky thing is that with the positive matter being cloaked with anti-matter the whole entity has zero mass and could be accelerated without effort, and this could account for the shuddering felt on the Solar Orbiter and the small jump observed on the shuttle, though I suspect that the ship may stay immobile in the rethe and the blue escape tunnel shifts to position itself around the cocoon. We haven't travelled faster than light but the anti matter exit mechanism makes it seem as if we have. The anti matter immediately prepares itself to eject the foreign invader. This would explain why those on board the Solar Orbiter did not experience terrific acceleration forces. I believe that the original course of a ship will be maintained and it will effectively arrive at the blue tunnel instantly and await an action to expel it from the anti- matter zone. I think that a blast on the rocket motors temporarily disturbs the cocoon and the net result is that the matter is ejected back into our domain, in order to maintain the equilibrium of co-existence. The only thing that has been bothering me is how we suddenly get into the black tunnel. The neutral zone boundaries are basically spherical and the entrance whirlpool seemed to orientate itself to be at right angles or near to it with respect to the direction of travel of the Solar Orbiter. Now with a gyroscope, if you push in a given direction then the reaction is to provoke motion at right angles to the initiating force. Imagine that normally if you were to give a blast on the rocket motors you would make no headway when nearing the speed of light, exactly as predicted by Einstein. However the black tunnels are actually gyroscopic whirlpools of gravity lines so if you press against them you could in effect create a sideways force field, and if the gyroscopic or plug-hole effect is greater on one side of the ship than the other you will move sideways and thence into the black tunnel. If by chance you went through the portal exactly in its centre the sideways force would not be generated and you would not be propelled down the black tunnel. The rocket motors on the ship were instrumental in achieving penetration because only they could apply enough force for the gyroscopic effect to occur. This effect was not possible with the gravity motor. This effect also explains how you get back out. The rockets push forwards or backwards and the gyroscope effect cause you to be ejected sideways back into real time existence. Remember that from our limited observations so far the ships reappear in our time zone exactly orientated as they were when they went in. Neither Captain Johnson nor the Prof ever remarked on this, but I will pull their legs when next I see them. Whilst in the cocoon Captain Johnson reversed his directional orientation before giving the blast on the rocket motors, but when he came out the ship was still orientated forwards and on its original course!

Now we will be limited in what we can do because the entry and exit portals are not everywhere but the whole thing should be like a car sat-nav system working only on postcodes. It won't take you exactly from door to door, but it will be close and you just travel the rest of the distance by a more conventional means. I must say that it may be years before categoric proof of these ideas is available but the main drift of my notion is that it should be safe, so long as nothing tries to break the cocoon in transit!"

"James, get this down you!" encouraged Helen offering the Whistler a large mug of steaming coffee.

"Well what do you think of that then?" he asked.

"As you know I am an intelligent woman, and I am not bad at mathematics so I can say that even though I have not studied your idea in detail, it all sounded good. Every thing observed so far has been accounted for. I suggest you sleep on it then publish without delay!"

James Whistler took a long swig from his cup, leaned back in his chair, let out a long expulsion of breath and murmured "well I trust I am right, because most of the scientific gurus I have asked are incapable of original thought and will only be interested in discrediting these ideas, which is all that they are at the moment. Bloody mental hunchbacks! I have expounded these ideas to you as they arose in my mind, nothing is written down yet, but I will let you be the first to read my documents once I have written them."

"When you have done that you must publish, you cannot in all conscience keep these ideas under your hat. But may I suggest that you look into a return trip to and from mars where you could pick up something from mars and bring it back in record time, as general proof of the operational success of the notion, and start off any lecture by telling them that you set out to achieve the final proof that Einstein's theory has *not* been broken. Call the jump function the sidestep function, a means by which you can appear to have travelled faster than light to all intents and purposes but that you have found a method of sidestepping the limitations existing in our real space time continuum! This may just be easier for your audience to swallow, and before you do anything else, ask the Prof to accompany you on any lecture tours that come up."

The Whistler grunted, smiled and said "I accept your advice Helen. By the time you are the Prof's age you may well be as wise as he is. Of all the possible people I could have chosen to unburden myself to, I chose you and I am glad I did. The other astounding thing is that the jump while in the anti matter zone still maintains your original course plot and the distance involved seems to be unrelated to time. So if your course on entry was aimed at say orbit round Saturn, you would be able to achieve that as quickly as say going to an orbit round Mars. Time has become almost irrelevant. Food for thought indeed! He pondered a little while longer, "you know it is as if we teleport the entire ship between two points in the galaxy, we uncreate time as it goes in and recreate it when it comes out. So in its solid form it does not go faster than light, but the whole exercise makes it look as if we have! Perhaps the Prof's notion that we had invented teleporting was in fact an inspired piece of supposition!"

He published as soon as he had edited his work, and then over the coming weeks, the furore started. His main opponent languished in a jail cell and was none other than professor Trueblood.

The Prof heard of Trueblood's intervention and wondered if Trueblood would make a good president of the flat earth society.

The Prof and the Whistler made lecture tours together, to each of the major seats of learning, the Prof made the introductions and dealing as only he could with occasional hecklers. The tour produced disciples and dissidents, the dissidents, who it must be said outnumbered their opposition, hanging onto Trueblood's interpretation, the adherents taking the Whistler's side.

The arguments raged back and forth in the press and articles ranged from the unbelievably uninformed emotional tripe to quite well reasoned notions. Finally the Whistler realised that he would have to put his money where his mouth was, and provide a demonstration.

CHAPTER 6

THE WHISTLER GOES ON A PROVING MISSION

The Whistler examined the locations of the recently charted black and blue portals and decided that a trip to mars was just about feasible, though the nearest blue hole was someway past mars and that the time taken for a round trip would only be between six and thirty hours depending on exactly what was done and most of that was conventional rocketry at each end, together with the acceleration and deceleration times of the gravity control motor.

Doctor Barry, remember him? was given command of the shuttle to be used and the Whistler went along as scientific advisor. Ken Lee on mars was fully within the loop, and he was asked to provide a container with something only available from mars to be given to the shuttle crew when they made rendezvous, and that only he would recognise when the container was opened back on earth. The experimental trip went without a hitch and the Whistler now was back on earth he attended a ready called pre-informed press conference.

He outlined the purpose of his mission experiment, as proof that the distances involved were coverable in very short time spans, and when questions from the floor had ceased, he reached behind him and produces a titanium container exhibiting the flag of mars, unscrewed the top and peered inside. His eyebrows shot up and he emptied the contents into his hand. There was not much in there and even the closest on the floor couldn't make out what it was.

"It seems to be a tooth!" smiled the Whistler. Communications with mars were already open, and Ken Lee was on the screen. The transmissions to and from mars were still very slow due to the radio waves having to traverse large distances, but after a few minutes Ken Lee smiled and pointed to the gap in his smile. "Removed only yesterday" he grinned.

There was an excited buzz through the room as even the hardest headed reporters realised that the Whistler had proved his theory to be correct.

There was no congratulation from professor Trueblood, in fact for several weeks he was on suicide watch, as he realised he had got it hopelessly wrong again.

New ideas abounded, the most major of which was from the communications industry, and they wanted to know if data transmissions could go through the rethe, thus speeding up communications. The Whistler admitted that he hadn't even thought about that and deflected the issue saying that research into such matters would no doubt be done, but it needed a team with the correct background to look into this. He added a note of caution saying that should anything be done to permanently upset the exact balance between the ether and the rethe, then we could all expect a cataclysmic big bang and that would be that so to speak.

In the expectation that the communication issue would be solved, the world space administration decided that for the moment all space travel would remain by means of the mark 2 gravity motor. In the event of an emergency requiring a rescue effort though, the new jump system would be considered as an option. The charts produced by Helen would form the basis of the charting exercise required for the rest of the Solar system, but there would be missions to bring the outer reaches of the Solar system within reach of the charting instruments.

The era of rapid space travel had truly begun, though the charting exercise was expected to take literally for ever. Each outward journey would take the adventurers to the limit of the present charts and thus a whole new charting era would begin, with the amount required to be charted growing as a cube law as the volume of charted space increased.

Helen restyled the charts for the rethe and drew them out in a similar way to the charts for underground rail travel. As she gradually refined her charting work it became apparent that any escape from the rethe back to the ether needed putting onto her rethe charts, and these would be provided with a real dimension location to mark where they were in the normal time space continuum.

She did not expect that there would be any gravity neutrals inside a large mass of material, and so it should not be possible to exit the rethe and find for example that you were somewhere in the middle of the sun, or other inhospitable place.

Because time was no longer an issue, she realised that any journey through the rethe was in fact a straight line, and that the charts could all be started from the same black tunnel. She decided that as there were numerous black tunnels within easy reach of earth, she could nominate certain explorations should begin from specific points, so that the routes to outer space would not be compressed into those for Solar system journeys. This, she reasoned, would stop the jump portals from becoming clogged. Instinctive common sense told her that if there was congestion it may cause an imbalance between the matter and anti-matter existences, and she was intuitively aware that prevention was infinitely better than cure, because there would be no cure only a big bang.

These off the cuff decisions were proved to be vital in later years with complex explanations as to why this should be so, but to Helen just at this time it was simply common sense.

The world was readying itself for the first jump mission. Where the devil would the mission go to?

Months of discussions followed with just about everybody wanting a say. There was however one phenomenon, still not yet explained. The apparent loss of normal control, by spaceships or presumably anything else close by, just as the jump was being executed.

The Whistler would not sanction the use of the jump for general use until he had an explanation for this. He was, as they say, a lone voice in the wilderness against a forest of loud voices wishing to proceed. The loud voices however were not head of space administration and thus the Whistler could baulk any such wild ideas as he saw them. Commercial interests however, sought to remove him from his post, and almost succeeded in their aims. Only the Whistler's reputation for being right when every one else was wrong saved him. Some of the board meetings that he attended were acrimonious to say the least, and only resumed the normal calm when the Whistler demanded that they replace him. There was no-one else with the necessary qualifications. Fortunately professor Trueblood tried valiantly from his jail cell to get himself installed as the new space guru, but all he succeeded in doing was in reaffirming the Whistler's place. Stupid as many board members were, they were not that stupid, and they did not want a political animal who was so far away from accepted thinking, that one board member proposed that the Whistler be given a vote of confidence, and then if the vote went the Whistler's way, a 10 year contract. The Whistler got his contract.

CHAPTER 7

ALL HAIL THE PROF!

The Prof knew that the apparent loss of control was a reduction in control and not total loss, and so he mused things over, and tried to think of a cause.

He started by outlining everything that he knew or wondered about, and he printed a list out from his computor, which went:-

1. Not total loss, rocket control still ok, but not very responsive
2. OK until the jump is in progress
3. More than one ship has observed this issue
4. Similar occurs on jump out as jump in
5. Therefore it occurs during transitions.
6. Does it occur as the jerk is observed?
7. Does it finish as the cloaking/uncloaking finishes?
8. Is it dangerous or simply a by-product of the jump?
9. The gravity motor seemed most affected.
10. Would the gravity lines be affected at the time?
11. Could anything other than the gravity motor be affected?
12. Time for another party!

Fast forward now eight days. The Prof asked Helen and the Whistler over for Sunday lunch, and it took them all that time to clear their calendars.

They took an early lunch and settled into the big comfy armchairs in the living room.

The Prof gave them each a copy of his print out and asked that each question be considered in the order he had written them.

1. Everyone was agreed that the lack of control had merely forced the ships to take longer to achieve their moves, it was also agreed that though the rocket motors were on dribble feed the moves had been primarily organised by other means.
2. They also agreed that as far as is known the normal manoeuvrability was available until a jump was in progress.
3. At least two crews had noticed the phenomenon.
4. These same crews had noticed the sluggish response at both blue and black portals.
5. They agreed that the sluggishness only seemed to occur during the transitional stage of the jump, and further noted that crews had said that the ships were almost locked when the plug hole effect occurred.
6. There was not sufficient information available to decide if the effect was there during the jerk stage of the jump
7. Agreement was unanimous that the effects all disappeared when the jump, in or out was completed.
8. There was no indication of danger but there was no contra-indication either.
9. The gravity motor was possibly not affected but the servo systems turning the ships on their axes seemed to struggle somewhat.
10. A deep study of the gravity lines was needed to ascertain what distortion if any occurred.
11. another investigation may be needed to establish other side effects if any

Now having gone through the Prof's list, the discussion descended or perhaps elevated itself to furious debates on each of the issues as each speaker considered them. They were well into the discussion when the Prof suddenly took a sharp breath and said "One of my electrical engineering chums told me about something called eddy currents. These occur when strong variations in magnetic fields occur around a conducting medium such as iron for example. The variations in field strength induce voltages which in turn cause currents, eddy currents to flow. Engineers take steps to avoid the generation of eddy currents because they always caused unwanted heating and unwanted magnetic fields and occasionally reductions in efficiency due to getting stray magnetic fields exactly where you didn't want them. This was common in electric motor design. Now as you know, I am not an engineer, so I could be well wide of the mark, but I wonder if there is some gravitational equivalent. If you could think of a suitable theory you could ask the engineering fraternity to predict the effects, and then you could mount a small mission into the ether and check the predictions!"

The Whistler's face suddenly went glacial, and Helen grinned across at the Prof, "you've set him off again!"

Several minutes later the Whistler emerged from his reverie. "Prof you may be wide of the mark on a purely technical level, but that notion needs following through. There could well be a side effect that causes a similar reaction to eddy currents, but I trust it will not cause heating, because if it does the rocket fuel may be vulnerable enough to cause a big explosion! If an explosion occurs while a rocket is in the rethe, it would be contained within the anti-matter cocoon, but the explosion would provoke immediate expulsion back into the ether and the ship may split into millions of bits as it re-emerged. We have to conduct a few experiments without delay! We must find out what actually happens as the cloak extends from the rethe to envelope the ship. It looks as if the plug hole effect is literally a gravitational whirlpool that induces some sort of reaction that slugs the movement of the ship. Eddy current magnetic fields react with the primary magnetic field and in effect can damp a response, and in the case of an ammeter can be used to stop the needle trembling. If there is a gravitational effect it is likely induced in the outer skin of the ship. If this is the case we can do conclusive experiments by trying both gravity motor and rocket motor moves! Prof you are the finest catalyst for new lines of thinking that we have!"

"Well, I'm just so clever," the Prof smirked.

Experiments have now been carried out and the effect was there irrespective of the mode of ship manoeuvre used. There was no detectable heating effect so the final obstacle to jump travel has been removed.

The space agency approached all likely commercial sources to raise the necessary backing for a full mission.

Many commercial interests were over ambitious in their wishes, but now that the Whistler had fought the good fight, so to speak, they would defer to his advice.

The Whistler laid down the following parameters:-

- The further most outreach point would still have to be on the charts.
- The mission would have to be of three ships; the first would go into the rethe and re-emerge before either of the others was to follow.
- The others would only follow when radio communication was re-established with the first ship.
- The second then the third would go with exactly the same rules to apply.
- When all three were gathered at the new destination, one ship would endeavour to expand the ether-rethe charts, another would explore wherever the destination was and the third would ready itself to provide aid if this was required.
- Both the Solar Orbiter and the Space Adventurer were available and within the month the Gravitas would be recommissioned after the earth space authorities had finished checking her over. Henrik Svensson would be commander of the Gravitas, Captain Cortez formerly of the Gravitas had accepted a desk job within the space authority and was to prove an adept communicator and would handle most of the communications between the space authorities and the commercial backers.
- The mission would be funded by all interested commercial parties, and with things being as they were, the mission would be expected to commence in two months time.
- The Whistler would offer himself as the scientific officer for the journey, and the space administration would be requested to set up a brand new holographic TV in the Prof's front room. He really was too old now to be considered for active duty in any

capacity, but his integrity and intelligence were still undimmed and it was agreed that he could still provide a valuable input.

- *NOTE from Catherine Whistler. I know this bit is boring but I can tell you as the spouse of a participant, I value the caution injected by the Whistler. I am so glad that the dissident voices did not manage to get his resignation. If they had I am sure he would have just given up and died, and he still has so much to give. I found out my grandad's full name and e- mailed it to the Prof. He was Edward Jackson Thyssen, so maybe our family has some roots in the middle of Europe. This is a surprise because I somehow imagined we had all come from England.*

The commercial wallahs agreed that the Whistler's basis was sound, even those whom he had fought so bitterly agreed that he had neither skimped nor gilded the lily. In other words they backed him whole heartedly. The Whistler diplomatically asked if any of the directors of the leading commercial groups would care to improve their knowledge of space technology, and take an observers role on the mission. One young man opened his mouth to say something but his boss quashed that idea immediately, so there was then a deep silence.

The Whistler smiled inwardly, as he now knew he was leading the meeting, and he hadn't finished yet.

He suggested that if some of the lower echelons within the commercial companies could be asked to volunteer, he felt sure that the companies would feel that there was at least one element in the mission who had their direct interests at heart. He asked for and got three young men, and after extensive interviewing approved all three.

These three were not known to each other and were assigned one to each ship. On the eve of the mission the Johnsons, Whistlers and Svenssons were all apprehensive, and they held another party at the Prof's. Henrik actually said a prayer for all those going on the mission and offered a toast to the 55,000 or so who made up the total complement of the three ships, realising that they together with their relatives would be in for a worrying time.

Henrik Svensson boarded the Gravitas as soon as he was able, and was warmly welcomed by his crew. One of the lower ranks begged him not to eject anybody into space. Henrik knew that this was a joke, but smiled inwardly and replied that as long as nobody looked like a mule he would be safe enough. He was also astute enough to realise that his reputation had preceded him and he then expected no dissension from his crew.

All interested parties sat round a table to decide where to send the mission. It was soon agreed that it would be the outer reaches of the Solar system, and favourite was the gas giant Neptune and her largest moon, Triton. Landings were not probable due to the cold temperature, but Triton was thought to be volcanically active and so may have a hot core.

CHAPTER 8

TRITON HERE WE COME

The early part of the mission was under rocket and gravity motor control and went without a hitch of any sort.

The Solar Orbiter was first off. She approached the first black portal and duly went down the plug hole. After a delay of about 3 hours a weak signal was received from Captain Johnson as he re-emerged from the rethe. Henrik Svensson was next to go and the Space Adventurer was nearby, observing. 3 hours later the weak signal was received from the Gravitas, indicating that all was well. Eric Whistler set his ship on the correct course and accelerated up to warp 0.95, arriving at the black tunnel exactly at the right moment and just as she went into the rethe there was a loud bang as something collided with the hull. The hull was punctured but the self sealing plastic triple skin quickly stopped any leak.

"Propulsion engineer report please!" snapped Eric.

"All systems go!" sir, came the reply.

"Life support team your report quickly now!" urged Eric.

"1.8 percent loss of gas through the leak sir, otherwise all systems full go!"

"Any report of anything unusual from any quarter?" enquired Eric.

Nothing was reported. Just at that moment however came a second resounding clang as the hull was punctured again, this time the self healing skin did an even swifter job of plugging the leak.

"All external lighting to full power, all cameras try to track whatever is giving us a hard time!" said Eric Whistler with a calm and crisp assurance that he really did not feel.

On screen suddenly one of the cameras picked up and tracked a meteorite. It was a piece of rock no bigger then a tennis ball. Spinning away from the ship, but suddenly it came straight back at them, but this time almost directly. This time it did not bounce off, but penetrated the triple hull and then came to rest in the weapons store. The hull resealed itself quickly, so no harm was done. The meteorite when checked was simple iron, with no traces of radioactivity, but it was quite hot. Fortunately it missed all of the cabling and pipework so this could be considered fortunate in the extreme.

"Resume normal stations!" ordered Eric.

The computor rang out the warning ejection alarm and fired up the rocket motors. Eric gave a blast at full power, and suddenly he was through, but was incredibly close to the Solar Orbiter, less than a mile between them.

"Space Adventurer reporting A ok. Urgent, request immediate three way head to head!"

"Granted" intoned Captain Johnson and the three musketeers met on board the Gravitas.

Captain Johnson inclined his head slightly upwards as he invited Eric to spill the beans.

Eric Whistler began, "we entered the rethe just at a time when a small meteor was about to hit us and it got sucked in as well. It bounced of the hull twice and was probably bounced straight back at us by the cocoon wall and the third time it penetrated and came to rest in the weapons locker. I have left my crew making good the damage and they should accomplish this in a short time. No damage to pipework or cabling has been found. Here is the offending bit," he laid the meteorite down on the table.

Both Kingdom Johnson and Henrik Svensson were deep in thought. Henrik spoke first.

"There were some odd small noises and we suffered a very small puncture, but I just put it down to a random collision with space debris!"

Captain Johnson pursed his lips and pressed his fingers together into a point. "The Solar Orbiter suffered no puncture, Henrik suffers a small puncture and you Eric suffered three punctures. We will send this data across to the Whistler, but I suspect that space around the chosen black portal was simply too dirty. Each action attracted some debris and you Eric being last, were at the greatest risk.

Now these punctures were the most serious that any space craft has suffered to date, how well did the self sealing work?"

"Here are some photos of the damaged areas, and as you can see the areas are substantial. The first puncture was this one here," he pointed at one of the photos, and we lost 1.8% of the atmosphere in circulation, equating to about 0.6 % of the total on board."

"Ok, it is pretty effective then, so long as we don't suffer another hit on the same spot, no problem. I suggest that replacement sections are fitted to the offending parts as quickly as is possible!"

"Agreed" said Henrik and Eric together.

"Right" said Captain Johnson, "every one return to their ships I will asked James to give us his thoughts on these issues before we go any further. Within the hour we should overtake Triton, but I suggest that we leave any exploration until we have done a detailed survey, so in effect we now have about a month to kill, unless Henrik knows a way to shorten the exercise!"

Back on earth Helen suddenly received data that showed her that everything was still on schedule and that all three rockets had made the jump successfully. She read with some trepidation of the punctures suffered and knew that she would receive a transmission from the Whistler before long. She offered a statement to the press without mentioning the punctures. The world was agog with excitement as the newshounds waited for more information to be forthcoming. Helen let it be known that the surveying work would take about a month, and trusted that the Gravitas would accomplish this without incident.

Privately she let Jane and Catherine know the exact state of play. All three women suffered anxiety pangs though they each knew that so far at least, danger was microscopically small.

CHAPTER 9

MAN'S FIRST ENCOUNTER WITH TRITON

It took 33 days for the charting exercise to be completed, and the ships crews could feel a slowly mounting excitement. During this time the Whistler engaged his mind into top gear as he pondered why the meteorite hadn't caused a spurious ejection back to the ether, and he tried to reason what would have happened if it had. He gave up after about a fortnight because he just couldn't amass any suitable data to base conjecture on. He did send via a secure link a holographic transmission to the Prof outlining his worries. The Prof sent a return message just saying "hmmm?"

It was decided that Eric Whistler's ship would mount the first landing on Triton, the other two ships would keep a watching role, but before the mission got under weigh the Whistler gave them some unexpected news.

Firstly from earth Neptune looked blue, due to the atmospheric gases absorbing the red end of the colour spectrum, only allowing blue light to be reflected back to earth. The mission was of course much closer then earth, and James Whistler had noticed a previously unseen phenomenon. There appeared to be a skin of some as yet undetermined gases on the upper layers of the atmosphere, and this skin acted as a fibre optic or conduit to the red end of the sun's light. The red light and its companion infrared, or heat as we know it, scooted round the outside of Neptune. The amount was relatively small, but it broke out from the skin on the dark side of the planet in the form of a converging beam that had suffered a total internal reflection. The focal point of this beam was at the correct distance to provide some heat on the surface of

Triton, when Triton was in the correct point of its orbit round Neptune. The first mission was to land on Triton near to where this beam was expected to hit.

The Whistler gave his grandson the co-ordinates and the away team commander fed them into his shuttle navigation computor.

"Shuttle commander requesting clearance for take off!" clearly sounded over the ships loudspeakers.

"Permission granted, good luck, and be careful!" replied Eric Whistler.

The shuttle eased away from the space adventurer and made its approach down to Triton's surface. The on board computor handled the entire exercise except for the landing, whereupon the shuttle pilot looked for and found a suitable flat space, then expertly landed. The landing spot was littered with small debris but nothing else of significant dimensions. The men all donned their heated space suits and the ground team duly set foot on the moon's surface, and found to their surprise that the suit heating had automatically regulated itself off and was providing no heat.

"Anybody uncomfortable with the temperature?" asked the scout leader. Each man indicated that he was not uncomfortable. The scout leader gave orders to his companions and they set about their tasks instantly.

"Scout leader to base, scout leader to base" he radioed.

"Go ahead scout leader" came the voice of the Whistler.

"The place seems to be warm!" ejaculated the scout leader, and it is bathed in a strange blue light, but anything white such as our space suit badges seems to glow".

"Well now who's a lucky boy then, I suspect that you have landed in the focal point of the guided infrared, and I suspect that if you move a few yards you will find it a lot cooler!" replied the Whistler. "The glowing observed will be due to ultraviolet light which is being radiated directly out of Neptune, take a few photographs so we can estimate the strength of UV radiation."

"We have already explored about half a mile radius and the place is still warm with the hottest spot about 200 yards from where we are standing" added the scout leader. "I suspect that the area warmed up must approach a couple of square miles!"

"Neptune's rotation is just over 16 hours and Triton is synchronous so it will be by my calculations, in the focal region for about 2 hours every 16 or so. Leave radiation and temperature monitors set up and running, get back aboard your shuttle and come to momma!" smiled the Whistler.

"Consider that an order!" spoke Eric Whistler.

"Aye, aye sir" intoned the scout leader, and within two hours the first mission was over.

During the debriefing of the away team, the Whistler suddenly intimated that another quick mission would be necessary because, it would be necessary to know the temperature below the surface. However the team leader grinned and said, "Well I already left them in place placed at one foot, two feet and four feet below the surface and in approximately the four main compass points, 12 probes in all approximate radius 40 feet!"

"Anything else?" enquired Eric Whistler.

"Yes sir I left two gas analysers running; only this time I did it on purpose!"

The whole of the space exploration fraternity knew that the breathable gases on Titan had been found accidently by means of gas analysers, but this was only the second time the perpetrator had admitted it openly.

"I suppose you could say that you learnt by your mistake" grinned Eric Whistler.

"It seems to be the quickest way to gain promotion!" grinned the scout leader.

"It certainly got you noticed this time" said Eric Whistler making a mental note from the guy's name tag.

"Keith Windridge" he thought. Then he puzzled as he found himself mentally allocating the name Brian Judd to the man. Why on earth did he think that?

The Whistler fed all of the gathered data into his computor terminal. Triton had a strange light dark cycle. It was on the bright side of Neptune for about 8 hours, but due to its synchronous orbit the hot spot as he thought of it, only got about two hours of daylight, but got it twice per rotation of Neptune. After that, about halfway between the two light periods, came the hot period of near two hours. When we say daylight this is really a technical point only. The sun was so small in the sky it did not provide much light but the effect was just about discernible by eyesight.

However there was what could be described as an earth shattering discovery just round the corner.

Captain Johnson revised his plan of attack and decided that he would give his crew a break from the monotony of aiding the Gravitas in charting the black and blue portals. He asked for and got approval from the Whistler, to mount the next mission, and he openly requested Keith Windridge as the scout leader.

The Whistler had already concluded that it was a good policy to erect one or perhaps two Eden shelters.

This second mission then used two shuttles, one from the Space Adventurer, and one from the Solar Orbiter.

To erect and secure the Eden shelters required some digging and as the men began to dig they unearthed some shards of a substance resembling glass. However when the shards were trodden on they did not break, they proved extremely strong and Keith Windridge expressed the idea that they may be diamond crystals.

The focus of the expedition had suddenly altered and the away team split into those doing the erection work and those doing the digging where the secondary task was to find and store as many of these shards as possible.

After the end of three hard days, the two Eden shelters were up and running with their life support systems in hibernation mode. The collection of shards was of immense importance because they did turn out to be diamond. Some pieces were almost four feet long and about 6 inches wide by 2 inches thick.

With the shuttles safely ensconced back on their mother ships, the Whistler got the metallurgists and materials experts to examine the diamonds carefully. The crystals were almost flawless and the size meant that for sake of argument primary compressor blades for jet engines could be made with strength characteristics, way above anything else so far seen.

Captain Johnson sent a coded message back to earth with the unscrambling key lodged only with the Prof.

The Prof raised his eyebrows at this discovery, and knew instantly that there would be an incessant clamour for another mission as soon this one was over, presuming they all got back ok.

Meanwhile Captain Johnson decided to split his mission where Henrik Svensson would use the jump to get near to Pluto. He was to survey Pluto exactly as he had surveyed Triton, then return after about three weeks.

Henrik was inwardly nervous as he had never been at the absolute forefront of space exploration before, at least not entirely on his own. In the event his mission went without a hitch and he suffered no more punctures to the hull.

Back on earth Helen found her stomach in a tight not which dispersed only slowly once she heard that the Gravitas had rejoined the other two ships. She had no knowledge of the diamond find.

Back with the mission Captain Johnson called a three way head to head on board the Solar Orbiter.

He also invited James Whistler into the meeting.

He served a good measure of whisky to each man, knocked his back and then began.

"Gentlemen this mission is almost over. For the first time we have made a discovery of massive commercial significance, that fortunately will mean other missions here and if I am not mistaken it will result in a small colony of miners being sent here. I think that we should undertake a charting mission before we leave to establish the size of the diamond deposits, and hopefully will show that this is not a flash in the pan. James can you add anything here?"

The Whistler took a second swallow of his whisky and smiled, "yes I think I can. On the original survey done there are one or two unexplained anomalies. These would be explained if there was a lot of carbon near the moon's surface. Diamond is of course one of the allotropes of carbon. I think that the local diamond field is about five square miles, and there are others but well away from the warm zone. If we mount a single mission down to the warm zone again we will have to dig down and see if this is just a surface phenomenon."

"Agreed" said all three captains in unison

"Further to that" added Henrik Svensson, "I think we should ship as much as we can back to earth as a taster so to speak"

The four men grinned.

"If that doesn't ensure the funding of the space programme, nothing ever will!" smiled the Whistler.

In the event the shuttles of all three ships ferried almost 25 tons of Triton diamond crystal. Some pieces were small like earth diamonds but there were many huge pieces.

"When a second full mission comes here we will have to do a lot more research before we come. If by some galactic fluke we have discovered the source of Solar system diamonds they make not take long to form, and the slightly ridiculous idea that we could farm them would be a rather splendid bonus! To date we had reasoned that diamond formed in the earth due to immense gravitational pressure and we found how to make small industrial diamonds by using the pressure inside a cooling crucible of steel. However I suppose that because some crystals can be grown, it is not beyond the realms of possibility that we could grow diamond crystals if the correct conditions are available. We may even be able to grow them into a predetermined shape."

Five days later the three ships were back in earth orbit and the entire crew were given indefinite leave, using just a few volunteers to keep things ticking over in between missions.

CHAPTER 10

THE PROF GETS A PRESENT

Captain Johnson used his connections on earth to machine some of the diamond into a walking stick. The stick was unbelievably light and strong at the same time.

When it was presented to the Prof at the next party held at the Prof's house he was, as they say, chuffed.

A curious reporter noticing the stick and hearing rumours of untold wealth being shipped back to earth put two and two together.

When the Prof was spotted out and about the reporter quipped "I see you've got yours then!"

The Prof raised his eyebrows and enquired "My what?"

"Your diamond stick," came the quick reply.

The Prof looked at his stick and twirled it round almost dropping it in the process and made a frantic grab to save it as it shot from his grip. "Yes, its amazing how good araldite is these days!"

With that he threw the stick towards the reporter who caught it deftly and realised he could bend it with his bare hands.

"Ah so it *is* plastic then" he shook his head but was convinced.

"You can keep it said the Prof I have two or three other prototypes at home, but be careful not to break it!"

And so it was that the secret of the diamond haul remained a kept secret for about three more weeks. In the meantime the bulk of the booty had been apportioned to the backers, though the space administration kept a substantial amount back for experiments.

"Clever boy is Captain Johnson," the Prof thought, "and that araldite red herring was actually quite a good stick, but not as good as the real diamond!"

The Prof had finally been informed of an unusual event during the homeward run and he had absolutely no idea what the cause was.

When each ship entered the rethe, the diamond sticks were seen to glow a deep blue colour, there was no detected radiation and the ships instruments did not pick up any traces of radiation or any other unusual occurrence. Every man who stood any where near the sticks though found himself staring at the beautiful gentle glow.

"If that effect could be found in the ether it would have a very profound effect on jewellery trades" the Prof thought. As it was, early fears about the effect of diamonds being fetched in from extra terrestrial sources did not blow the industry apart. The price of diamonds had always been kept artificially high by starving the market, and in this instance the same primeval forces were just as efficient as ever. The small amount of extra terrestrial diamond allowed into the market place simply whetted the appetites of the buyers. These foreign crystals were so near perfect that it did not take as much skill to cut the facets into the stones, but the prices remained high so that the status quo of the market in diamond jewellery remained virtually untouched.

With such a sudden reward for their investments, the space venture backers outbid each other for the privilege of being part of the action and the space administration acquired a wealth beyond all expectations. Quietly the whole aspect of space exploration had changed. There were scientific theories abounding that described the behaviour of the rethe, and some would no doubt be good enough for consideration on or before the next flights. The space administration became the Microsoft of its era, the wealthiest scientific/engineering body on earth.

The building of another ship was commissioned; the design being a virtual update of the Freeloader, this ship would set up a route between earth and the Neptunian system though it was decided for safety reasons to proceed a little further on gravity motor to a cleaner black hole. This turned out to be nearer Venus than earth, but with the jump being so quick the distance and time to get there was a small proportion of the overall mission time. The ship was named as "The Moneybag". Say no more.

A regular supply of diamond crystals kept arriving

Earths materials experts soon found a way to melt the diamond crystals and join them up into long strings. These were then rolled and pressed into steel girders, giving a simple solution to strengthening buildings to withstand earthquake tremors and or explosions more easily, and on the personal transport front, a very thin lattice of diamond could be made economically and was slowly being incorporated into the safety cell in family cars. This added appreciably to the rigidity of car body structures, and thus aluminium was used for many car bodies and less weight provided better acceleration and far greater fuel economy. Taking into account the fuel additives derived from Titan, the earth's own oil would now last for almost a millennium more and the pollution emitted had now reduced far enough to allay the worries, well founded or not, about greenhouse effect.

No matter how good an advance is, there will always be those who will decry it as being insufficient. None other than our old friend professor Trueblood was instrumental in organising the dissident movement, still from his jail cell. This time however he was onto a loser from the beginning, and those complaining voices slowly ebbed away and became lost in the background.

The only thing left to do now was to take a leaf from the Startrek series and go boldly forth.

The Whistler knew that it was time to take this unprecedented gamble but it was a huge step to consider. It would have to be done with volunteer crews, and he did not feel easy about asking for volunteers, particularly as he knew no way of assessing the effect of rogue space debris going through the portals, and as yet he had no way of establishing communications from in the rethe to in the ether.

"This damn job I have is getting bigger by the day" he thought. He picked up the phone and tapped in a number. Then tapped in several other numbers, as the transmissions got through he was presented with a number of holographic images at the same time, a ragbag of voices greeted him. "Time for another party" he growled, I suggest 28 days from today, oh, and no children this time, allow three days."

The Prof, and the others at their terminals had never seen the Whistler so grim and determined before and they all agreed to the date, and the unusual request to make a three day hole in their calendars. Giving their children a summer school holiday was the method used to free themselves up and the kids who knew each other well enough by now departed on the due day eagerly.

CHAPTER 11

THE NEXT PARTY

Fortunately modern high speed glass tube rail services were that good that surface travel across the globe was well established and rivalled air travel for overall speed. Some of the partygoers had to travel over to England to get to the Prof's place. The Prof always tried to avoid these journeys himself as he found them tiring, and the others loved the peace and tranquillity offered by the Prof's home and were happy to make the journeys themselves. They all arrived within an hour of each other, and the Prof gave them a typical English breakfast. These formalities over the Whistler outlined his worries.

"Firstly" he began, "I do not know why the meteorite that penetrated the Space Adventurer did not cause a spurious ejection from the rethe when it hit the wall of the cocoon. If it had caused a spurious ejection the ship would not have been lost but it would not have rejoined the other ships in the same time frame. This could of course not be a total disaster but it could pose difficulties in completing the mission. I suspect that it could have ended up a fortnight away so to speak."

He paused.

"Secondly we cannot proceed until we have cracked the issue of communication. At the moment we can get to a destination before the radio signals transmitted as we enter the rethe do, and this anomaly will have to be sorted." He drew a breath.

"Thirdly, we have now been to the extremes of the Solar system and have found discoveries not expected. We are colonising mars, we have a prison and various other facilities on Titan, and these are both self sustaining operations. We have had a good look at the Jovian system, and really I do not think that there is likely to be anything else of similar use to earth. We have got a fantastic result from the Neptunian system and we have charted space well out past Pluto, but then come the regions beyond the Solar system. We have no charts and no means of getting them unless we go outside the Solar system. If we do go boldly forth to borrow a phrase from the trekkies vocabulary, we have no idea how to get back. We could end up living on the space ships until we perish of old age!"

A silence pervaded the room and a certain sense of gloom prevailed.

The Prof cleared his throat and said "well Catherine have you heard any scuttlebutt that might give us a clue as to how to proceed?"

"Me?" I was startled by the question. "I am a librarian not a space scientist, so you can't take anything I say as meaningful!"

"I beg to differ" smiled the Prof. "I heard you say that you had picked up a rumour that the diamond sticks glow red on the outward journey to Triton!"

The Whistler sucked in his breath sharply as he got the drift of the Prof's thinking. "Catherine, if this is true, then it may be that these shards glow blue when we are travelling to the sun and red when we are away from it. Now whether or not it would still work when we were light years away is another issue but it could at least be used as a homing beacon inside our own system!"

"I am not in the habit of going into pubs on my own. I am not my Grandad. Even in these enlightened times, a woman's motives are always suspect if she starts chatting to strange men in bars. I did however hear a couple of guys from Henrik's ship saying this when Eric was away getting me a drink in a restaurant one night! I haven't even mentioned it to Eric, but the Prof somehow gets me to spill beans I didn't even know I'd got!"

"Thank you Catherine," said Henrik, "but how do you know he was from my ship?"

"A bit of guesswork really, he had a Gravitas cap on!"

"Henrik thought for a moment, and then said "I think I know who that man might be!"

He excused himself from the table and made a mobile phone call. Ten minutes later he was back.

"I have arranged for this man to travel to the rail terminal about 20 miles away I will wait for him there and bring him here blindfolded. After all we don't want to compromise the secret location of the best runner beans in the world do we?"

The Prof shot out of his chair and scampered to the kitchen. He came back into the room and said "panic over I hadn't even lit the gas! Dinner will be served about half an hour later than I intended."

Henrik stayed for the dinner, after all he may have had Nordic roots but he had acquired full English palate and couldn't resist sampling another of the Prof's roasts. It turned out to be cottage pie but a la Prof.

Three hours later Henrik returned with his crewman.

"Right ho then Keith, tell all about the colours!" murmured Henrik, "what you have done is a petty thing not an ejection issue!"

Able spaceman Keith Windridge looked uncomfortable and held up his hands in surrender. "All right, all right, I know I shouldn't have done it but I found a shard of that diamond substance when I was clearing up the mess left in the cargo bay, and I took it to stop somebody else pinching it!"

"Well that has got to be true" gasped Henrik, "no one would offer such a paltry excuse otherwise! And why are you known as Keith Windridge and not as your real name which is Brian Judd?"

Brian Judd acknowledged the question with a nod but continued, "After I had taken it I was seconded to another part of the ship for a fortnight and when I finally got back to my quarters, I had had it too long for a simple explanation, and I didn't fancy a term in the brig. With the next batch I simply put it amongst the cargo as soon as I got the chance, and I thought that was the last of it, but while I had got it I noticed that it was a deep red, almost invisible to the naked eye, as we were making the outward jump. The glow persisted for a few seconds after we came out of the rethe, but I didn't hold on to it for long enough to find out if it illuminates before we had actually made the jump in. I suspect it might though."

"What exactly are your qualifications Brian?" asked Captain Johnson.

"Crikey, Captain Johnson, sir! Sorry sir, I didn't notice you at the back. I am in general engineering. It is a wide discipline and we are asked to solve many problems. There are always experts on every subject, but it is guys like me that get in there first, and we often predict the likely cause of the trouble and then bring in the experts, and they take all of the credit!"

"Yes I am afraid we do!" cut in the Whistler, "and I can tell by your general attitude that you are an asset to the space administration. I can see that you are of a practical disposition. It was you that suggested the easy way to repair the puncture leaks in the diamond mission was it not?"

"Oh crikey, the Whistler as well! Erm yes sir it was. I had looked at the design and I could see the designers intention was to fix a large man sized gas proof box internally around the hole, with a suited man inside it then simply unbolt and twist the component to bring it into the ship, and follow the reverse to put the new one in. I couldn't imagine they ever intended that a man had to do a spacewalk to fix it and I just thought that it would be safer, particularly whilst in the rethe."

"Have you any idea what would happen to any one who ventured outside into the rethe" enquired the Prof.

"No sir, no idea!"

"Good because neither have we!" added the Whistler "so why the two names?"

"My mother used to worry due to a family incident from years ago and so I invented the second character so that if I somehow got into the news she wouldn't worry about me. My wife knows all about my little subterfuge, but she is the only one other than me who does, and I am gobsmacked that somehow you all seem to know! But back to space things, I must say sir that when the puncture occurred my superior officer was ordering the repair to be carried out by means of a space walk, only moments before we returned to the ether."

"Eric Whistler joined the conversation at this point, "It will need to be drummed into every section leader, that only on direct orders from the Captain and the Second in command in unison must anyone be sent outside into the rethe. We have no idea what dangers this would bring and therefore it must be avoided at all costs! Gentlemen, an aside if you please!"

After a few moments hurried conversation, Eric Whistler turned and added "We have just decided to add a new rank to the space service and this will be a specialist rank within the general engineering fraternity and will be Hull Integrity Officer. If you accept it, you will be the first to hold the rank!"

"Brian Judd's mouth formed a cheeky grin as he said "What's the pay?"

"I should think about 30 % more than you get at the moment would be appropriate" chuckled the Prof, as he looked at the Whistler for confirmation.

"Yes I think that should do. The rank would give you authority over all of the general engineers in matters concerning the hull and should be stipulated as to how many men you can second without requiring special agreement with section heads." The Whistler nodded then added "Mr. Judd, erm Brian, you do not lack self confidence, so tell us, how did you ensure that we would hear about the crystals changing colour?"

Brian Judd smiled and said "I had no idea who or what to tell. All I did was mention it casually to one of my drinking mates when I was off duty. It must have spread from there!"

"I am sure that in future we would prefer to hear it first not last" chimed in Henrik. "Now if I may I would like to introduce you around everyone here just so that you know the right people to tell if you make any other earth shattering discoveries."

Brian Judd was a little embarrassed but shook every hand that was held out to him and gladly accepted the invitation to stay for tea.

As they were sitting down to the evening meal, he looked rather awkward and asked if he could phone his wife who would be wondering where he had got to.

Henrik then smiled and rang a bell on the table, and in walked a fresh faced woman looking rather flustered. "Nadine!" spluttered Brian.

Always the charmer, the Prof had already pulled out a seat for her next to himself, and asked her to put aside any fears she may have because her husband was being feted as the man of the moment.

"What has he done?" She squeaked.

"I think I may have invented or discovered a sort of galactic loadstone or compass "Brian said.

Quietly the Prof felt his respect for this man growing as he had an excellent grasp of the practical but had enough technical knowledge to act as a link man to the scientists. A bit like himself.

Nadine blossomed as the evening wore on and it was obvious that she was a woman of some character, with a barbaric sense of humour that she brought to bear even on Captain Johnson making him laugh out loud.

"Brian Judd stood and proposed a toast, "Even today it is not what, but who you know and then who knows what you know!" all glasses clinked and Brian added, "I fear that we must leave you now or we will miss the last train!"

"The only place that you will be going is to the third bedroom upstairs on the right interrupted the Prof, you will be needed here tomorrow and then it will be a company chauffer driven car that takes you home, Nadine has already seen to your children."

"Brian Judd squirmed with delight and embarrassment in equal measure as he suddenly realised that his chance in life had unexpectedly come straight out of the blue.

He exchanged a glance with his wife and sat down in a strangely numbed state.

Nadine looked at him and glancing round the room, said "well you have managed to shut him up, and I have never managed that! Brian I think I may be guilty of blowing your cover. After your mom was ill I am sure I mentioned it to the local priest. I know it seems impossible but I think it must be that. After all how else could Captain Whistler have heard about it?"

Eric Whistler could not remember where he had heard about it, but he did recall looking at Keith Windridge and yet mentally thinking Brian Judd.

Shortly after that the Judd's took their leave and went to bed. The others discussed many things and the discussions went on long into the night.

At breakfast the next morning Brian Judd was talking earnestly with the Prof, who suddenly said "tell that to James Whistler!"

Brian began "It suddenly struck me in bed last night that if this idea actually works, diamond crystals should be mounted in the gravity motor shield system, then wherever you are, seek out the blue glow by turning the gravity motor servos and then you know you are on the right orientation as soon as the crystals glow blue. Not only that with the amplification factor at its maximum you should be able to seek the sun out from far away outside the Solar system. I've got a feeling that at the dawn of creation these diamond crystals were formed and are somehow part of the sun itself and will always act as homing media, not very scientific but it's what I think."

"We shall have to conduct more experiments and see if we can activate the crystals in the ether, because if we can then we will have a new tool to aid our homecomings. Outside our Solar system, it may be possible that the crystals will find the primary form of central gravitational pull at the centre of other stellar systems, and if this works we really would be able to consider far, far missions and as they say go boldly forth. The crystals could of course display other colours according to the direction of travel and all this needs to be checked out thoroughly" said Captain Johnson.

"Gentlemen" broke in the Whistler, "enough of the shilly shallying, we must proceed with our experiments without delay. If the crystals do not work as hoped then we will need another attack, but in the meantime I must say I am expecting a result. Fortunately the space administration for the first time in its history has sufficient funds to proceed without using the begging bowl. From this moment everyone at this meeting including you Prof, and all of the ladies are under a security blanket of silence. Please do not let this get to the press or anyone else! Helen you are our usual link to the outside world these days. I think you can admit that the Prof is testing out a diamond walking stick but that he is recovering from a badly cut leg caused by a simple trip up."

"That should occupy their imaginations, for a while!" smiled the Prof, do you know that in one of our national dailies my photo actually replaced a page three girl. I'm not sure whether to be flattered or insulted!"

Brian Judd was not finished yet. "I think I know why the meteorite did not penetrate the cocoon wall" he began then paused, he had the attention of every one in the room. "Well it just wasn't big enough. The cocoon has to have the strength to shroud a spaceship having a mass of many thousands of tons and the more positive matter that goes into the rethe, then the stronger the protective field around it must be. It would cause total internal reflection of any small loose items and after a number of bounces it would be bound to force the object to head for its epicentre, where the ship would be. So it may have come in at a funny angle but after several bounces when it likely missed the ship, eventually it hit it and once the ship not being so perfect a medium as the cocoon had suffered one bounce it would alter the angle and path of the loose object. This would mean that any loose object was bound by Newton's laws to end up on or in the ship."

The Whistler shook his head almost in disbelief because he knew that there may be other as yet unknown forces at work, but he thought that Brian Judd was right. "Brian, we top scientists occasionally get too embroiled in the large picture or in some small detail and we fail to see the middle picture. You are I am almost certain, right in principle. If you are wrong then I will be surprised. For some time now we have relied upon the Prof to kick our thoughts back on track and it would seem that you and the Prof are kindred spirits!"

Nadine for once was silent as she realised that her faith in her husband had been born out in spectacular fashion. Many of her friends thought that Brian was a bit "off the wall" so to speak, and he probably was. This ability to go along thought paths that simply do not occur even to the most intelligent people in the world was a valuable commodity and she began dreaming of a modest improvement in their lifestyle even though fame had not yet come their way. She knew though it was only a matter of time. She felt an inner glow of deep satisfaction and was instantly sorry that Brian's mom had not been present to see developments for herself.

Brian was still not finished. "If you want to waste loads of money trying to get radio signals through the rethe, then go ahead but any first year student could tell you it simply won't work. For every radio transmission ever made they all went at some frequency or other, and in the rethe there is no time, so something required to operate at so many cycles per *second* simply is not possible"

The Whistler had not applied himself to this problem at all and if he had he would have arrived at the same conclusion, so he knew Brian was right. For the first time he looked worried and said "well surely we cannot have advanced ourselves to a point where we can transmit solid matter quicker than we can transmit radio signals have we?"

Brian continued, "Well you invented faster than light travel not me, and the only solution I can see is to send solid messages. If you can't convert radio signals into and out of matter then I think you will need a ship allocated to permanent jump duty. You could record all of say a two hour transmission on a memory stick, transmit it to a similar stick in the jump ship and send it back. When it came out of the rethe back near earth, it could squirt its data to a ready waiting decoding ship and then return to mother. The signals would then be transmitted back to earth in real time and the jump ship could cycle round and round and provide two hour squirts every two hours if required so that from earth's point of view the transmission would seem continuous."

The Prof took up the thought, "If you decided upon a number of jumps out into the far reaches of space, you would need a succession of transmission ships and you would be able to use them in much the same way, but ultimately you would run out of options and you would then be blind. It is all very well going boldly forth, but you must have some way to come boldly back as well!"

Brian added that this system would not be cheap because each jump ship would cost a fair bit and would in essence be a relay pigeon, and to conserve rocket fuel would only go into jump mode when requested by a command from the mother ship. Thus there would be a fair bit of metal out in space largely in a quiescent state. For a triple jump you would need three relay ships. Perhaps when procedures became established it may be possible to get wherever you wished making only one jump, but for the moment the space service couldn't encumber itself with a one jump system."

The Whistler who was chairing the meeting, brought matters to a close saying "I can see that we have a number of things to do, and I don't want us to get in front of ourselves so Helen and I will decide on a co-ordinated programme to explore the various possibilities. Thank you ladies and gentlemen for your input, and remember walls have ears! Perhaps you could all think of some fancy name for the proposed transmission system as you could well imagine the reaction I would get if I tried to sell the notion of carrier pigeons to the boards of directors of our backers! The meeting is officially closed and after the next gargantuan feast that the Prof has ready and waiting I will arrange for company chauffeurs to pick you all up at different times during the day, and from a few carefully chosen pick up points. Ok that's it and I have one small apology to make, Brian I'm sorry about the blindfold, but until we were certain of your attitude we have to be careful, a left over from the mule's day I assure you."

Brian smiled and dipped his head in acknowledgment. Nadine was talking to Jane and Helen, who remembered how it had been said at Helen's first party when she had said "what a swell party this is." Nadine agreed that a more apt phrase would be hard to find. The women got on extraordinarily well. This was one of the qualities looked for by the Prof as he knew that one awkward woman could have surprising and detrimental influence on the morale of any sizeable enterprise.

He did find a strange kinship with Brian and felt assured that he could now really relax as many of his own skills were found residing in Brian's mind.

CHAPTER 12

THE WHISTLER'S LIST

The Whistler made a list of tasks to perform, which was as follows

- Mount 6 diamond shards in the gravity control nose cone
- Perform experiments to see if the glow can be initiated in the ether
- Try a live experiment on board a shuttle style ship and report on the details of any glow seen. This would involve trips in the ether and the rethe and Brian Judd was to be given a significant role.
- Construct a compressing programme designed to compress speech for use in radio communications into and through the rethe.
- To design suitable modems for modulating and demodulating the radio signals

The first bullet point was dealt with within the week. Brian Judd was asked to select 6 shards and oversee the fitting into a shuttle type craft.

Brian chose four almost perfect shards and two not quite so perfect. He arranged them in parallel in a forward pointing triangular form, and similarly in a side ways pointing direction. He made sure that each shard was interchangeable with its neighbours.

Within two days the shuttle was placed on a trolley on the ramp and the ship was accelerated up into earth orbit. Brian wasn't certain but he thought he saw faint traces of orange or yellow during this period. He asked the Captain to get the ship up to about warp factor

0.8 and checked again. There was no visible light emanating from the shards. He asked the Captain to do a 180 as he put it and the captain duly obliged which involved slowing right down then accelerating back up and informed Brian of the new velocity when attained. There were no glowing shards but Brian had seen something during the process. He requested the Captain to slow the ship right down to as near zero velocity as possible and checked his shards once this had been done. There was a distinct if dim glow a definite yellow.

Brian was excited when next he asked the Captain for a manoeuvre. "Please maintain zero velocity, but orientate the ship a full 360 degree turn in the horizontal plane" he requested.

The Captain not quite used to his use of the word horizontal out in space, still managed exactly what was requested. Brian was busy camcording the shards. "Please now execute another full 360 but in the vertical plane!" again he camcorded the results and scribbled furiously on his notepad.

"Thank you Captain, most excellently done, please now orientate the ship to point directly at the sun, still at zero velocity. Ok now open the gravity window for forward motion with maximum acceleration. The characteristic hum occurred and the shards all glowed blue so brightly that they lit up the gravity motor room. "Thank you Captain, reduce speed to zero again and orient the ship directly away from the sun then full acceleration please!"

The Captain complied and this time the crystals glowed as if red hot.

Brian asked the Captain to make a jump through the nearest safe portal and then back again, and he specified the course coordinates to be taken up before the jump.

Brian knew that this jump would take him into an unexplored region near Uranus and told the Captain this. The captain was no other than our old friend Doctor Barry, who raised enquiring eyebrows at Brian.

"The object is to see if the glow is brighter or dimmer when we are far away" said Brian.

Doctor Barry complied with no fuss and the whole experiment was done again.

"Brighter or what?" asked Doctor Barry.

"Considerably brighter," said Brian, but they are at their brightest when we are in the rethe.

Doctor Barry then asked why he hadn't asked for an orbit round Uranus because that would give all directions with regard to going to or from the sun and would likely be a manoeuvre done by space captains out in the field.

"Why didn't I think of that?" smiled Brian. The orbit chosen gave a six hour cycle time and the memory stick on the camcorder just about had enough memory to film it all.

"Ok Captain, when that is done, search for the nearest plug hole and then let's go back to earth!"

The camcorder showed a variety of colours according to the travel direction and glowed brightest when the gravity window was open and the amplification was turned up to maximum.

Brian Judd knew he had enough material to provide a teaching demonstration and decided that he would complete that before presenting his work to the Whistler.

In the event when he went to make his presentation, the Whistler had been dragged out of his beloved lab on commercial matters. Helen was the first to see the little presentation and she was sharp enough to grasp the basics within seconds of him beginning. She said "right, it works when the ship is stationary or is at its best when accelerating hard from rest and the colours glow according to your direction vector."

"Absolutely correct" said Brian impressed by her quick grasp, "but the beauty of it is that it is quite visible at normal rocket speeds and so will be a practical guide. The only thing now is to go outside the Solar system and see if my theory holds up there. I've already seen the glow much brighter when we were near Uranus so I know it's a possibility. It is just like a small baby separated from its mother, the further the separation, the louder it squawks! In point of fact I now consider the shards to be gravitational detectors, and they only work when they are subject to the gravitational acceleration, with no other forces acting effectively upon them. I have found that if you tie a cord to one shard and whirl it about your head, then a just discernible glow occurs, and though I do not have sufficient maths to prove anything, I think Doppler shifting can also be detected, though where Doppler Effect would be expected to give a red shift, we get a blue shift!"

Helen in her turn was quietly impressed with his work. He really did seem to have that Prof-like quality when there was absolutely no evidence to go on, his first guesses seemed to be spot on. Brian had in effect covered the first three bullet points on the Whistler's list.

Brian would take a back set for a while now as the transmission engineers tried to provide a suitable system for compressed data. The Whistler knew that the military had used compressed data transmission as far back as the short but effective Falkland's war in the latter half of the 20ᵗʰ century, and possibly even before that.

The Prof knew a number of retired electronic wizards and approached these on behalf of the Whistler. A team of older men was assembled many of whom already knew each other. With a team of space researchers at their beck and call it wasn't long before the first compressed system was up and running. Within a few short weeks the team had perfected a system that scrambled and unscrambled, compressed and decompressed, and used a extremely high frequency that was only any good over about 500 miles even in space, so that the amount of digital memory used was surprisingly small, and conversely it was possible to contain about three hours speech on one chip. An approach was made to the computor microchip industry and they further introduced the system of zipping much loved in the industry and costs were kept to a minimum. The system devised was no use on earth, the frequency was too high for use in an atmosphere and even transmitting to and from a satellite was unreliable, but out in space it suffered none of the earthly setbacks.

A shuttle loaded with the decoding modem was launched and made to sit motionless in space a few miles from a blue exit tunnel. Doctor Barry's ship was used and sent to Neptune on its jump.

The communications jump ship was carried aboard Doctor Barry's ship and when launched was loaded with a message ready for sending back to earth. Just at this time someone had told Brian Judd a rather good if racy joke, and he split his sides with huge guffaws of laughter. Doctor Barry decided on the spur of the moment to use this laughter as his transmission message. It was squirted across into the communication jumper and at the same time transmitted back to earth by conventional means. The comms jumper as it became known was remotely set on its journey and accelerated up to warp 0.95 arriving at the black tunnel just at that moment. They had found that it was not necessary to shut the gravity motor down, just give a good blast on the rockets. The characteristic plug hole swallowed the jump ship, and moments later it reappeared exiting the blue tunnel. The decoder ship received the message in compressed form as the jump ship hurtled past, and then re-orientated itself as it sought out the black portal in order to return to its mother ship. The message transmission back to earth exceeded all expectations, and the listening crew was astonished at the clarity of tone.

"Somebody's told Brian a good one there!" quipped one of the crew who knew him.

Back on earth the Whistler also listened in and could also hear the comments from the listening station. He was delighted that the tonal quality was as good as the best HIFI he had ever heard and that Brian's laughter was so recognisable. The Whistler settled to wait occupying his time researching mental patterns used in the determination of certain mathematical problems. He was disturbed from his reverie after a further two hours or so by the arrival of the standard transmission. There was a background noise but Brian's unmistakeable laugh was there to be heard. It was time to go public, any time now there would be demands to do as the trekkies did and go boldly forth. He knew he would have to go on the first such venture just to give the crews some confidence in the mission. Every where on earth, he was known for his reluctance to rush off into the wild. He was known for his cautious and measured approach. In his head he did not feel that confident and decided to call for another party at the Prof's.

Note from Catherine Whistler and Jane Johnson. We can feel it coming and we are powerless to intervene. The little boys who are our husbands are behaving in very tense and unaccustomed fashions. There is a party called for at the Prof's and we are going. We are worried.

CHAPTER 13

THE FAREWELL PARTY

Just the day before the party, all of the children were given a grand surprise party by the moms. Children were not invited to the Prof's do, so it was only fair. After that they were given a day out at auntie's or uncle's or grandad's houses as the case was for the individuals.

The parents could all feel a rising tension and even the charm of the Prof was unable to alleviate the gloom that was felt.

The Whistler stood after the latest of the Prof's glorious meals and tapped the side of his glass with a spoon.

"Ladies and gentlemen, I can tell from the atmosphere at this party that you are all in a despondent mood. This mood is misplaced. Let me re-cap the facts to you. Just a few years ago right at the beginning of space flight as we have come to know it, everything, but everything was unknown. We had sent probes to the outer reaches of the Solar system, but that was all. Captain Johnson here commanded the Freeloader, and she was a brand new design using a brand new untried form of propulsion, and yet every crew member aboard the ship knew they were going completely into the unknown, but with very little anxiety. Ok, ok, perhaps this was in part due to ignorance. We are less ignorant now and we have concluded exploration as far as Pluto. Now that is a very long way from earth. With the present three ship arrangement we will have the proven ability of two captains and a commander of the utmost skill and integrity, together with Brian Judd who is our latest find so to speak." He raised his glass and said "I give you the final frontier except that there isn't actually any frontier unless we make it!"

The glasses were raised and sips were taken, and some small smiles showed.

Realising that morale must be raised if the mission were to have any success at all, the Prof stood as the Whistler sat down.

"Ok you idle, good for nothing scroungers, I am informed that whilst on this mission all senior ranks will get double pay, further to that all lower ranks will get double and a half!

I suggest that when you make your first jump out of the Solar system, that only one ship do this but send a comms jump ship back immediately and then the others to follow after ensuring the comms link back to earth has been established. I further suggest that the decision as to who goes first is done by a coin flip, odd man out going first."

This simple suggestion noticeably relaxed Jane Johnson as she realised it could still be her husband but not now for certain. She was still worried but only the same as Catherine Whistler, Helen Svensson, and now Nadine Judd.

Conversation began to flow and the very fact of speaking of worries was seen to diminish them.

Eric Whistler spoke up, "You know it isn't quite the same for we men, but we don't like leaving our loved ones and our young families any more than you ladies like to see your men off on a Boy Scout jaunt!"

"When you make the jump, what are you looking for and where are you expecting to find it?" asked Jane Johnson.

Kingdom Johnson gave forth on his innermost thoughts, "we will not be looking for life, but we will be looking for another earth or mars, as to where this will be I don't know. As the most senior Captain here, and still being in my prime, I imagine that the heaviest responsibility will fall upon me. I have no orders yet, but I am sure that this is the way things will be. What I propose to do before we send anyone off on this jump is to use a spare comms jump ship and programme it to out reach some great distance and then make the jump back. We already do this purely for communications and therefore we can use it as our pathfinder probe. Some weeks ago I asked Helen if she could generate a laptop programme that could begin the mapping of outer space, and she has managed to do this. I propose that this be sent in our probe and when the ship returns we glean whatever we can before any half cock jumps purely into the unknown. Believe me my first concern on all these missions is for the safety of my crew, though I freely admit that safety of my own crew did not enter my head at all when we achieved our first accidental jump. I was thinking purely of the crew of the Space Adventurer, and believe me I did not expect to achieve a jump, it just happened when we turned the final stone so to speak.

"I think he loves me!" grinned Eric Whistler, and suddenly the remaining ice melted away and the Prof noted with some satisfaction that the combination of the personalities involved had as much to do with that as any crafty psychology.

Later in the evening the Whistler took the Prof aside, and told him that he had been doing some personnel research. The Prof listened as the Whistler told him of a chance connection he had made between two space service members. He told of the earth quake that had taken the son of one man and how the man's wife had been desolate and had never recovered finally succumbing when only in her late forties.

The Prof sighed and said "that was me and my beloved Mary was it not?"

The Whistler agreed that it was. It was the earth quake issue that had enabled him to make this connection, and he revealed that a man in the earth quake had lost both his parents in the quake, and that man was at the party.

"Brian Judd!" exploded the Prof.

"According to DNA records he is your son!"

"I knew there was something about him, and I saw that little scar behind his left ear, but I didn't dare to hope" mumbled the Prof as he looked around the room with wet eyes.

Just then Brian Judd walked over and said, "you've got nothing in your glass dad!" to the Prof. The Prof burst into tears, and the Whistler said as he watched Brian gaping at the totally unexpected response from the Prof, "Brian may I introduce you to your father?!"

Brian Judd was staggered, but before he could protest the Whistler told him of the DNA comparison.

Brian Judd just said "I wondered why I liked him so much!"

He and the Prof stared disbelievingly at each other, then capitulated and warmly embraced and the two men brought each other up to date with a little of their lives since the quake. It would take many months even years of talking to fill all of the gaps. Brian fetched Nadine across and she fought the tears that threatened to engulf her as the situation was revealed.

"The one thing our kids always said they missed was not having a Grandad like everybody else, and Brian never gave up hope that his parents could have survived that quake."

The Prof quietly realised that he had acquired a family, and not by marriage or adoption but by true blood line. He really had something to live for now and suddenly felt the extreme pangs of worry experienced by the women at the party, and yet also felt something primeval, an answer to his unspoken prayers.

"I fully understand your worries now ladies, and any or all of you will be welcome here at any time, don't wait for your husbands just come with your kids, and you Nadine he said as he hugged her with astounding force for an older man, I shall expect you at least monthly!"

CHAPTER 14

THE MISSION GETS UNDER WEIGH

Henrik Svensson, Captain Johnson and Eric Whistler each spoke in turn of the hopes and fears for the forthcoming venture. Captain Johnson summed up all of the ideas that had come from this meeting and decided that Eric Whistler would be the wing man. That is he would accompany the main mission though at some distance to one side. Henrik Svensson would make the first jump, which would be to Pluto, in the Gravitas. The Solar Orbiter would act as link man with Captain Johnson carrying the Whistler on board. As the Gravitas re-entered the ether the Solar Orbiter would launch the spare comms jump ship and it would be programmed on a pre-decided course defined by the Whistler, and would enter the same black portal as the Gravitas but on a slightly different course. As soon as possible after that the two veteran captains would make the jump as far as Pluto and join Henrik Svensson. Captain Johnson stressed that the plan was not set in stone but should be adhered to unless harm would result from so doing.

This part of the plan went without a hitch, or so everyone thought. Henrik Svensson had broadcast to his entire crew including the undercrew that the slight shuddering felt was caused as they entered and exited the rethe. A cheer went up as every man and woman realised when they experienced that, that they had in layman's terms exceeded the speed of light.

One engineer then arrived on the bridge travelling at almost Olympic speed on his space boots. Trying to draw breath he nodded his head at commander Svensson. Henrik moved quietly to one side and tilted his chin at the engineer who stood before him.

"Sir, the ship may have experienced a slight judder, but the gravity motor central core almost shook itself from its mountings. There is an easily repairable buckle on one of the servo racks, and with respect sir I recommend that it is both repaired and investigated immediately!"

"Thank you Mr. Patel, go and sit in the inner bridge room and await my further instructions" said Henrik rather curtly. Within a short space of time the ships radar registered the presence of the Space Adventurer and the Solar Orbiter. Eric Whistler was first to break radio silence and as his ship was middlemost he requested a head to head aboard the Space Adventurer.

Twenty minutes later Eric Whistler was joined by Captain Johnson Henrik Svensson and Ravi Patel.

Henrik noticed Captain Johnson's one eyebrow rise as he saw Ravi Patel. He said nothing until they were ensconced in the inner bridge private room.

"Ok Henrik what gives?" started the senior commander. Ravi told them of the massive vibration seen in the gravity motor support servos and of the bent but repairable rack. Eric immediately asked his propulsion engineers to look in their gravity motor room and to report anything unusual. Five minutes later the communications channel sputtered into life and the flashing lamp told Eric that the secrecy function was in operation.

"Bridge here, report please!"

The Space Adventurer's engineer reported exactly the same problem in a calm and matter of fact way.

"Mr. Patel, were you in the gravity motor room for one jump or both of them?" said Captain Johnson.

"Both sir, as far as I could tell the inward jump caused some small damage but this was severely exacerbated by the outward jump. It occurred to me that the Judder frequency was very close to the natural frequency of the servo motor installation and as such caused very large vibrations!"

"I suppose we are going to need some clamp system to hold everything in place during the jump. Our engineers can soon have something in place in say about three or four days" said Eric Whistler.

Henrik Svensson said, "I don't remember anything like this on my last charting flight to Pluto, but I suppose the damage could be cumulative. I suggest that Ravi visits all three ships and gives us a detailed report for comparison and digestion."

"An excellent idea Henrik, I further suggest that we ask the entire crew if anything, no matter how small, has come to the attention of anyone. We are about to embark on a jump into the unknown, so everything must be in apple pie order. We are not hamstrung by a time schedule so we must proceed with all caution." instructed Captain Johnson.

Just then the inter ship communication channel blipped on, and Brian Judd's unmistakeable face filled the screens. "Two communications just received; firstly you may be pleased to know that we have received a very weak signal from our guinea pig comms jump ship. She appears to be ok and is executing her change of course to find another black portal so she can return to us. The second is from earth and concerns Commander Svensson." He paused.

"Well read it out, they can hardly relieve me of my command can they?" smiled Henrik Svensson.

"No Captain Svensson they do not want to do that!" smiled Brian Judd.

Captain Johnson smiled and offered his hand in congratulation to Henrik. "I don't think the mule would have given you that!" he grinned, "all you need now is a space ship to captain otherwise you will be stuck as a commander!"

Henrik compressed his lips to try to hide the smile that was upon them. He failed. "If I was on my own ship" he said "you would all have a whiskey in your hands by now!"

As if by magic within literally two seconds the filled glasses appeared.

"So that's why you were so quiet Mr. Whistler!" joked Henrik, taking a good swig, "come on now don't forget Ravi here!"

Ravi professed to be a teetotaller but had a small glass, and spluttered as the hot liquid burnt its way down his throat.

"How on earth do you drink that stuff?" he grinned, "mind you I suppose that we are not on earth are we?" he sipped the rest of it more slowly.

CHAPTER 15

WHAT ON EARTH ARE WE LOOKING FOR?

After repairs and strengthening of the gravity motor servo racks and the inclusion of a clamping system, another head to head was called, this time aboard the Solar Orbiter.

Captain Johnson chaired the meeting, and began by asking the question outlined above.

He added "Well now we are still earth men and by that I mean that that is where we regard as home. Possibly it may be that spacemen will evolve, but I don't want us to just wander around the universe looking for nothing in particular, as true spacemen might.

We may find other rich sources of minerals that we can tap and if we do then there is every chance of further missions to exploit them. We are a manned probe/explorer and we have already found low forms of animal life on Titan and the ingredients of life on Europa.

We know that the life of our sun is not infinite though that limitation will affect no-one in the foreseeable future. I think our mission is to find hospitable worlds where mankind could live, so in the event of some mule like nutter causing, say, irreversible pollution, we would have a chance of re-establishing the human race elsewhere, other than Mars.

The latest information from the Hubbell telescope is that a number of other planets have been detected, and I have a direction vector to get to the nearest. We do not know where our blue tunnel may place us exactly but I propose that all three ships make this first jump one behind the other, but I will send a jump ship through first. The mission will stay as a close knit group unless circumstances dictate that we would be better off split up. Questions, anybody?"

Eric Whistler was the first to jump in "I think this is a statement rather than a question, but presumably we could find ourselves in another Solar system and there could be planets within easy reach. If we find one where the solar energy per square yard equated to that received by earth, then we should investigate, and if there is a good supply of water then we must investigate!"

"Henrik, you have a contribution?" asked the mission commander.

"It is about now when we could do with that lifeform detector as operated on Star Trek, but I suppose that if we find this haven we will be bound to make land fall, though that would seriously deplete our rocket fuel tanks if shuttles are not refillable from their mother ship."

Captain Johnson picked up the mission communication transmitter, and asked for Brian Judd to report to the bridge on the Solar Orbiter.

"Brian Judd here Captain, I am aboard the Gravitas just now, but I could be with you in say 20 minutes!"

"Ok Brian, bring your discs on the rocket fuel systems for the shuttles and the mother ships if you please!"

Shortly there came a knock on the door and in walked Brian Judd smiling. "I think you are considering using the mother ship for frequent and full refuelling of the shuttles, are you not?" he began.

"You really are the Prof's kin, second guessing our requirement so easily," grinned Captain Johnson.

"To be truthful sir, I have been pondering this issue for some time. The concept of the shuttles would give them a good reserve of fuel for the foreseen uses, but I imagine that these are now meant for planet fall rather than moon fall, and accordingly would require a replenishment of fuel during a mission. Fortunately there are drain-holes, plugged of course, fitted to each of the main fuel tanks. We could tap into them to provide a bowser connection, and we have sufficient pipe work aboard to do the task. However there would be a requirement to take the fuel line on the outside of the ship to get it to the shuttle bay without causing immense disruption to the general running of the ship. The pipes used would operate at low pressure out in space and would thus not stress the pipes used. I took the liberty of presenting my idea to the pipe service engineers, and they have offered no objection. In case of unforeseen issues I would recommend that two ships be converted in this way but the third be left alone. This would leave one ship exactly to the original design and would leave her with a full complement of fuel on board. The other two ships would, I suggest be at their missions end when the main tanks were down to half full. The path proposed for the pipes would not require them to cross the rotating part of the ship, and would not run any risk of contaminating the canteen or toilet areas."

"Eric Whistler looked around the room and said "Well I doubt that there is anything to add to that! I imagine Captain Johnson would wish for the modifications to be carried out immediately, as I would if I were the commander!" Captain Johnson nodded in the affirmative.

"Would the team like me to compose a suitable announcement for the crew, as they would be stricken with fear if they saw all of the work going on without any explanation" chimed in Henrik.

"Brian, I think you must proceed with all possible speed, take as many men as you see fit, after all it will find work for idle hands just at the moment. Henrik, compose the statement, I will make the announcement as soon as I have seen your words, and now I think that a pint of mad hatter would go down well!"

They all trooped off to the canteen, and made a show of the jollity that they felt.

The following day the loudspeakers all boomed out, "this is Captain Johnson speaking, the shuttles are to be provided with a refuelling system on the Gravitas and the Space Adventurer, and so that we will always keep them well fuelled when we are further into our venture. It will be required to use the shuttles as planet landing craft, and just to ensure that each time we use them they will start with a full fuel load, more frequent refuelling could well be required. Even as far away as earth is, it has successfully detected other planets and we have the co-ordinates to make our first real jump into those areas of space. All three ships will make the jump in quick succession. The shuttles aboard the Solar Orbiter will not be refuelled in this way, but will have a hospital function in case of emergency. I will advise all members of the crew when the jump is imminent, and the day before the jump, beer and food rations will be doubled except for those working on the fuel piping system. Their rations will be trebled, thank you all Johnson out!"

He smiled as he heard the cheers reverberate throughout the ship.

Thirty two days later the ships all had their jump co-ordinates loaded and were ready. The jump ship went through first but no communications were established, even after eight hours

CHAPTER 16

OFF INTO THE UNKNOWN

Captain Johnson reasoned that the jump this time was so far that the pathfinder jump ship simply didn't have a powerful enough radio transmitter on board to make itself heard, and anyway they really had no idea just how far away the jump was, only that it could be several Solar systems worth of length. He boldly decided to press on.

Each ship entered the rethe on schedule, and each crew member felt the slightly giddying effect as the ships moved into the rethe, and then back again.

Captain Johnson took a minor risk; he broadcast his messages to the entire crews of all ships.

"Gravitas report in please!"

"Gravitas here, all systems functioning, A ok" replied Henrik Svensson.

"Space Adventurer here. No problems to report. We have the jump comms ship ready for whenever you wish to report back to earth!"

"All ships please conduct a space survey of the area within measuring distance. Put the records on disc and report to the Solar Orbiter with them. Use space shuttles for the journey; do not attempt the use of personal propulsion packs at this juncture! Captains to remain on board their own vessels, send senior personnel of your choice on this small mission!"

Five hours later Captain Johnson had all of the three discs to survey and James Whistler was called in for his opinion on the findings.

The Whistler displayed all three discs simultaneously on the computor screen and compared each to the other very carefully. He combed through the records and this took him the best part of four hours to complete.

"If you don't mind Captain, I would like to ask Brian Judd for his comments," he murmured.

"Problems?" enquired Captain Johnson.

"Small anomalies only!" smiled the Whistler.

Two hours later having gone through the anomalous parts of the surveys with Brian Judd, he asked for his comments.

Brian Judd asked for the exact relative positions of each ship, and then he proffered his view.

"Our ships seem to impose a slight distortion on the surveys of their companions he said, perhaps we should use rocket power to move away for an hour or two and then redo the survey in the affected areas!"

James Whistler considered for a moment and then nodded and raised enquiring eyebrows at Captain Johnson.

"Ok, I propose to leave the Gravitas where she is and the others will proceed by rocket power to a distance of 200,000 miles, if that distance is deemed sufficient?" he raised his eyebrows in turn and gazed across at the Whistler.

Quick calculations were done and the Whistler and Brian Judd or "Judder" as he was becoming known answered simultaneously. "That should reduce the influence from its present level to only about 0.01%, effectively! Now just one thing- is that small satellite just visible over there not our probe jump ship?"

It was and this relaxed a hitherto tense crew. The jump pathfinder was gathered and taken on board again.

"That move is agreed." The ships began their moves, during the lull in other activities Captain Johnson suddenly said "What's all this about being called 'Judder' then?"

"In essence it is history repeating itself. My dad became known universally as the Prof, just from things he said and the same thing has happened to me. I was standing in the canteen when we made one of the jumps and as the ship shuddered slightly. I commented that the judder was nothing to worry about. Well from that moment someone called me Judder and the name spread at phenomenal speed, and I think I am stuck with it now!" even you had heard of it Captain Johnson and I know it won't be long before you will say something like 'well what do you think of that Judder?' need I say more?"

"Ok Judder, we will do that," grinned the Captain.

Quietly the Captain knew that the similarity in personality between Judder and the Prof was quite noticeable and he felt a sudden sense of security that had been lacking when his old friend the Prof had decided to retire. He thought to himself "The first on board row we have, I will ask Judder to sort it out. That will test his Prof-like qualities!"

When the revised surveys were done the Whistler could find no fault though he did notice from them that the blue and black portals seemed to be larger than in the Solar system. From this he reasoned that the system they were in at present was several orders greater in size than the Solar system. He knew instinctively that he was right about this, though there was no scientific way of verifying things just yet.

At this point Captain Johnson decided to make his first report back to earth. He sent an uncoded message over to the Space Adventurer, with instruction to send the comms jumper back to rendezvous with the earth bound comms jumper, and to advise when the comms jumper returned.

Only 90 minutes later the comms jumper was safely back on her harness on the Space Adventurer, and it brought a congratulations message back from earth. The comms system was working! He had no way of knowing whether or not the earth bound comms jumper had successfully completed its round trip, but he knew the next attempt at communication with earth would soon show that up. So far so good! The probe jump ship had meanwhile been reclaimed and had suffered no discernible damage.

"Mission command to Space Adventurer and Gravitas, close ranks again, come close enough for visual detection please." He watched as the two ships moved precisely to their stations, and the fleet gathered speed.

"Mission command to Space Adventurer and Gravitas; here are the co-ordinates for our next jump. We will go Orbiter first Gravitas second and Adventurer third. Please acknowledge!"

Both ships immediately responded, and at the calculated moment the Solar Orbiter used rocket motors to force herself into the rethe, a large very fast item appeared from nowhere and was headed directly at the other two ships.

"Jump" shrieked Eric Whistler as he powered his rocket motors to full power.

Henrik Svensson was also screaming the same words as he did like wise. All three ships entered the rethe almost together. Captain Johnson was alarmed and staggered when he heard the other two ships conversing over the communications systems asking if every one was alright.

He recovered his composure, and butted in "what the hell is going on?"

Eric Whistler was the first to reply "literally just as the rethe swallowed you up, a large fireball about the size of sonny at Mars came hurtling directly at us. It was going at a terrific speed and I screamed to jump as I hit the throttles. Henrik was also screaming the same as me and he is in the rethe just behind me, but I can see the Solar Orbiter Captain!"

"We are literally in the same boat, I think," grinned Captain Johnson. "A five way head to head with the Whistler and Judder is required the moment we are back into the ether!"

The outward jump was incident free.

The meeting was held aboard the Gravitas. Four of the five men were excitedly jabbering about their near escape. Then Judder spoke up.

"Gentlemen, immediately prior to the jump there was no sign of any spatial body in our vicinity. This fireball appeared after the Orbiter made the jump. Thus the conclusion is clear, the fireball was already in the rethe and breaking into the rethe cocoon let our unwelcome visitor out. Looking back now it is possible it would have only skimmed us, but I for one, am glad it was decided to jump into the same pool as the mission command ship. We have now established that communication is possible inside the rethe, at least within a single cocoon, and that it is possible to enter and exit safely as a group. I think that the blue portals and black portals are different to within the Solar system; I think that the gravity neutral area had at least one of each. If the fireball had not escaped then it would probably have fried the Solar Orbiter unless the exit had been made very quickly. I don't fully understand this time inversion function that the rethe has, but I could do with a whisky!"

Henrik was already at his cupboard and he offered a good slug to every one on the room saying "We should broadcast to the crews that we have successfully made a triple jump, that is, we all went together and this was necessary to avoid a sizeable piece of Space debris."

James Whistler had considered Judder's notion and then spoke out "OK, we should do what Henrik says, and that will keep the crews well up to date. I think that we were so far from the suns of this system that the fireball would now be on an orbit taking thousands of years and so it should be ok to reuse that portal on the way back. That fireball could have been trapped right from the moment that this galaxy formed, and I think it was shear bad luck that its orbital course nearly wiped our mission out! In future we must send in a pathfinder jumper while we are some distance away, and anything trapped in there would explode out, and miss us or at least give us some escape time. I did note before we entered the rethe that there is a binary star at the centre of this galaxy, and that there is one planet that seems to have a figure eight shaped orbit and goes round both suns. There is a gap of about 40 million miles between the suns. There is an orbital period of about 30 years for the suns themselves, but the planet I am interested in takes about four hundred days to do its entire orbit round them. This place could be like earth, thus not quite unique, so as a scientist I feel like an eight year old boy who has just found his pile of Christmas presents before Christmas!"

"Well does it have to travel between the suns on its orbit?" asked Judder.

The orbit is nearer epitrochoidal actually smiled the Whistler, if you remember the rotary internal combustion engines, the periphery of the rotor used to go in that fashion."

"Hmmm, yes I think I see. The planet will gather speed as both suns pull it and it will be drawn closer in by the combined gravity. When it gets past the halfway point though it is moving away from one of the suns and so it is then going that fast that it takes up a wider orbit, as it proceeds because only one sun is fully effective. The same thing happens on the return part of its orbit so it will look similar to a figure of eight!"

The Whistler smiled and said "Brian, I have been up at nights trying to figure the maths of this orbit out, but just like your dad you have got it about right!"

"Time for another communiqué back to earth so Eric would you please begin to set that up I will have a report ready for you first thing tomorrow, meanwhile gentlemen, one for the road?" Captain Johnson was already looking forward to the near future and this gave him a certain mild thirst for good quality alcohol.

A silence ensued as each man was lost in his thoughts as he sipped. Then Brian spoke up. "Captain I know that Catherine Whistler and Jane Johnson will be amongst the first to see the reports back on earth. And I would be staggered if Nadine doesn't come a close second. Can we put a time element into our messages so that earth would know full details if we are lost but, if we are not, then, the narrowness of our recent escape will not be common knowledge?"

Captain Johnson pursed his lips as he considered this. "I think not Judder; I think you may be forgetting Helen. As the Whistler's number two we cannot hide anything from her and if she knows, in spite of her legendary closed lips policy, the other women would prise it out of her and that I think would be no good thing. Request regrettably denied."

Judder was surprisingly philosophical "ok Captain, I see that you are right--- as usual" he grinned.

The Captain however couched his communiqué in as matter of fact terms as he could, so that all relevant facts were there but all emotionally scaring sentiment was stripped out.

NOTE from Catherine Whistler. When Jane and I read this latest communiqué there was absolutely nothing in it to scare us, so why are we scared?

CHAPTER 17

ALL TOP LEVEL MEN AND SECTION LEADERS ATTEND THE MISSION PLAN DISCUSSION.

The canteen aboard the Solar Orbiter was used to discuss and plan the next mission.

The Captain unusually had a sheet of paper with notes on it; he referred occasionally to these during his discourse.

"Gentlemen, order please!" He waited for silence to fall. "I have asked you here for your input and of course to explain what the general plan of attack will be when we set out from the flotilla with a view to making landfall. What some of you may not know is that Eric Whistler has taken the Space Adventurer out to the next planet on this binary stellar system. This planet was observed to be almost as cold as Saturn though it is not a gas giant. There is water there in abundance and it is frozen absolutely solid. Whilst he was away on that mission Henrik Svensson was in the Gravitas on an inward journey and there are five lumps of rock further in. The two innermost are restricted to elliptical orbits and only go around one sun. The next two do follow the figure of eight shape and Henrik's mission was to observe these planets. Both of these planets are too near the suns and are inhospitable. We are thus constraining our mission to the planet nearest to our present position. This planet maintains an orbit some 100 million miles from the centre between the suns, and its mass equated to about one point two times that of the earth. There is liquid in great oceans on the surface but that would be no good if it turns out to be nitric acid or some such other corrosive substance. The power of the two suns is comparable with the output from our own sun. The effect of this on this planet seems to provide about a thirty two year cycle going from hot when both suns are seen, to cold when one sun partially hides the other. We do not think that this effect is extreme, but the planet has an axis tilt of some thirty degrees and so winters and summers are more due to this than their suns' cycles.

I propose that we send a manned mission and set up an Eden shelter. I further propose that we go fully armed. So far deaths in the Space service have been no higher than normal mortality rates for an enterprise of this size. I do not wish recklessness to cause us to deviate from that record. Surface atmospheric pressure is about half again as high as on earth and the gases it contains may prove to be breathable, but this has yet to be established. Now I know the little boy Adventurer in all of us wants to rush down there and get on with the exploration.

However, I order right now that the senior commanders of each vessel remain ship bound until more information is gained. I expect to be inundated with volunteers to go, and believe me the character of the volunteers will be vetted thoroughly.

From the planetary survey carried out by this ship while the others were checking other planets, we can say the following: - We can see the conditions for sustenance of life are there, so we may see nothing, or dinosaurs or people of accomplished intelligence. We simply do not know. There does not appear to be any artificial lighting during the dark periods, so make what you like of that. The planetary rotation is about 25 hours so it is earth-like in that regard.

If our first Eden shelter succeeds in remaining viable, then we would add to it to create effectively a small village.

In the longer term we expect to try plants, but of course once on the surface we will be looking for water. We need water and heat to survive so the original landing team will need as wide a group of basic survival skills as possible. Now only one at a time please, with your questions!"

There was an absolute silence from the floor, which lasted for about thirty seconds then the questions began, slowly at first and then more enthusiastically.

Finally Captain Johnson stood once more and the floor hubbub died down. "I trust that the answers we have given may satisfy your curiosity for the moment, so I expect you all to go back to your stations now and digest what you have learnt here today. As from tomorrow those wishing to be considered for planetary exploration, will all be considered. Please, leave your name in the register computor on the far table. Remember our primary duty is to get back home in one piece so we have no room for loose cannons. Go now and consider!"

The usual muted but excited babble broke out and the crew members slowly filed out, some of them pausing to tap their names in the volunteer page of the computor register.

CHAPTER 18

PLANET FALL AT LAST

The selected crew of the away team was headed by our old friend Heinrich. The mission was timed to arrive at dawn and the first footers were on the surface just as the light began to strengthen. Every volunteer noticed the gravitational effects as being oppressive, even though they had not been in space long enough to become fully accustomed to weightless losing their strength as a result. The main parts for the Eden shelter were unloaded by the time the first of the two suns began its rise. Heinrich called a halt to their labours so that every one could witness the sunrises. The first sun to rise was bright and yet somehow weak and was reminiscent of the sunlight on earth during a partial eclipse. The landscape was raw and new looking and the team could see liquid in the not too far distance. After half an hour the first sun was still not fully visible when the second began to rise. There was an immediate strengthening of light and heat as at this part of the cycle the second sun was nearer than the first. The sunlight itself was slightly reddish although this turned out to be due to the atmosphere and not the suns themselves.

Work restarted and construction began again. Heinrich marvelled at the ingenuity of earth's engineers as the clever but simple structure rapidly took shape. The work to erect this shelter took two and a half planetary days.

So far there was no sign of any life. Heinrich asked for volunteers to trek the presumed 3 miles or so to the liquid lake/ocean or whatever it was, and on the third day, a side arm carrying party, set out on foot with standard food and drink packs.

The party was gone until after dusk and Heinrich was worried even though he had been in regular radio contact. Finally the exhausted adventurers made it back to base camp.

Heinrich allowed them ten minutes to freshen up and recover then asked for details of their findings.

Jack Robinson spoke out, "well this planet is twenty percent bigger than earth, but believe me the distances involved to get to the liquid were deceptive. The terrain is not easy going on foot, some of it is just slightly soft, other of it had enough scree and rubbish to punish your feet and with the greater gravity we made slow progress." He reached inside his breast pocket and placed a phial on the table. "I really think that that is water, though it may not be potable to us just at the minute. I offer this to the lab boys, and each of us has a similar sample taken from points about a mile apart in each direction from my central sample.

More important however is what I think I saw, which my colleagues did not. Whilst they were away fetching other liquid samples, I looked out and I saw something rise then disappear again rather like a fish or reptile, I am not sure. It was only a glimpse, but maybe we have discovered another Loch Ness monster!"

Heinrich considered this for a moment and took the cup of tea that was being offered to him, and he nodded to Jack to drink his. They drank via the straw pipe fitted to their helmets.

"Jack, I want your combined report absolutely as soon as possible. Include every detail, no matter how small; the future conduct of away missions on this planet could depend on it."

He was halfway through writing his own observations up and he had noticed that there did not appear to be any plant life at all, though the landscape was quite colourful.

During a lull in the mission the weather changed. There was a sky covering that he knew was cloud. It didn't look like cloud it was green-grey rather than the puffy white he might have expected, but it produced rain. He sent several men out just to catch samples and when analysed, these turned out to be pure rain water. This was an important discovery and before he could stop him, Jack Robinson whipped open his visor, and drank his sample greedily.

"Jack!" he barked, "Visor!"

Jack blinked and coloured up, but by then he had taken several lungfuls of the planets atmosphere. Heinrich rushed across and snapped his visor shut, just as Jack crashed to the floor. Ten seconds later Jack came round and said "sorry sir, being in here, I simply forgot that we haven't created an atmosphere yet, but I must tell you that I feel alright! I panicked when you shouted at me, and I realised what I had done!"

Heinrich beeped the communications channel and got a response from Henrik Svensson.

"One of my party has just accidentally taken about 30 seconds worth of local atmosphere into his lungs. I know this is against all current advice, but he does seem to be ok. He fainted at the time, but I think that was just panic when I shouted at him. I think we are just about finished here for the moment and I intend to set up and leave a gas analyser running to provide information on the contents of the atmosphere. I will leave its sampling pipe protruding through the wall so it will be outside the Eden canopy!"

"One moment please, ah they are all asleep. Ok be it on my head perhaps, but you have my permission to return to the mother ship, Svensson out!"

The ensuing three days were all spent analysing the results and the oceans were probed as deeply as they could for any signs of life. There were none at all detected. The gas analyser was checked on numerous occasions, and sure there were gases there not present in earth's atmosphere. There was some helium and in spite of helium's lightness it was detectable at ground level. Nitrogen still made up the bulk of the atmosphere and accounted for almost 90 percent, leaving only about 7 percent for oxygen, and 2 percent for nitrous oxide and others.

"James is it breathable?" Eric asked him.

"Basically not detrimental to us but whether or not we could breathe it and live in it, I really wouldn't like to say!" smiled the Whistler, mind you I didn't think we could breathe the thin Martian air but we are adapting to it. I remember Grandad taking his helmet off on mars, and the old sod was 100 years old. Mind you he didn't try it for long! Perhaps we should ask for volunteers and select the youngest and fittest and proceed with a programme gradually increasing the exposure and noting any side effects."

Word soon got around and there was a plethora of volunteers even from amongst the undercrews.

Back aboard the Solar Orbiter Captain Johnson mused over the progress so far. He discussed his thoughts with the Whistler and Judder.

"I feel optimistic that we could mount a permanent expedition here, though I am sure that Jack Robinson was not mistaken in spotting something living in the sea. I notice that plant life has been found in the sea and I dare say it would evolve onto the land under its own power. I must confess that I actually have an ulterior motive just for once. As soon as the Prof found out our mission was a certainty, he gave me these." He fished in his pocket and brought out a polythene bag full of runner beans.

"He is a megalomaniac; he wants to start a bean empire," laughed the Whistler, and then uncharacteristically he went into peals of uncontrollable laughter.

"I really needed that" he gasped, "I see no reason why we shouldn't try to cultivate them, and if they show signs of reasonable growth we could try any or all of the shipboard seeds, we have ample to spare, the on board farms do ok so I think that we could risk that. I don't think that we risk contaminating the planet, so why not give it a go?"

Captain Johnson suddenly smiled and agreed.

Within two days the beans were planted. Fourteen days later the green shoots appeared and then they grew lustily. The soil if we call it that was of course completely virgin and had had none of the sustenance taken out of it by other plant life.

Encouraged by this, a true farm was set up and a number of additional Eden shelters were constructed, though one was deliberately built upside down as a trap for rain water.

The amount of oxygen was too little to provide comfortable breathing but one or two people found they could live in it reasonably easily, so long as they were not very active.

By this time the mission had been ongoing for six months, and confidence amongst the crew was high. The planet was nearing its winter point now in their hemisphere and it was appreciably cooler. The Whistler and his team did their best to predict the temperatures over the whole of the cycle and due to the steeper degree of inclination they knew that the winters may be quite severe, and the summers could be very dry and hot. The Whistler predicted that the reason that there would be no natural plant life was due to the extremes of weather.

Separately each of the ship commanders was allowed a week down on the surface, and Eric whistlers motorcycles were adapted to the environment. The spot chosen for the landing had not been chosen at random. It had been carefully selected, and it really looked as if it would be possible to colonise the planet from such a starting point.

A store of food stuffs large enough to support fifty folk for five years was shipped down and stored in a specially constructed bunker, and then volunteers were interviewed for the privilege of staying on the planet, as early colonialists.

In the end nine men and nine women were cross matched and selected for the team. The colonialists were already garnering the crops they had planted, and so imagined that they could become self sufficient in a few years time. A fully fuelled shuttle was left on the surface suitably sheltered near to the Eden village, along with an exploration and sampling vehicle.

A small programme of exploration was given to the settlers, and they were keen to find out as much of their new planet as possible. Captain Johnson decided a date for the return and each mother ship calculated its jump co-ordinates. All calculations were triple checked, then off they jolly well went.

CHAPTER 19

THE RETURN TO EARTH GOES UNEXPECTEDLY WELL, AND THEN.....

The ships all approached their black hole at different times and went through without incident. When, once again, on the outer edge of the Second Solar System, as it was to become known, a check was made on the location of their fire ball companion. This was still hurtling away and would continue away for half its orbit time. This was a little over 16000 years, and after that it would be another 16000 years before a revisit was likely.

The ships then lined up ready for the penultimate jump into the Pluto area. This was done and the first of the comms jump ships was reclaimed and stashed on board. The final jump had a blue hole somewhere near Venus and the whole mission reassembled in venutian orbit. The first sign of any problems was the lack of response from earths radio stations, absolutely nothing was available at all.

Judder asked if he might borrow a shuttle and go into earth or lunar orbit to try out his mobile phone.

Captain Johnson agreed and a shuttle was dispatched with Heinrich and Judder on board.

Once into lunar orbit Brian called Nadine and was delighted when she responded almost immediately. "What's going on down there Nadine?" he asked.

She spoke urgently and told him that she had almost given up hope of ever hearing from him again and said "there has been a terrible war. The Space administration has been disbanded and all those who worked there were being hunted down and imprisoned. I have Helen hiding in our loft. Helen has managed to secrete away all of the Space administrations funds, and she is public enemy number one at that moment. You have when all said and done been away for three and a half years, and things can happen in such a long time span."

"Ok Nadine, our records show we have been away for eight months, so there is some updating to do. Right at the moment our ships are in orbit around Venus. Do you know if the Freeloader is still operating?"

"Yes the weekly runs to mars are still going as far as I know!"

"Ok see you as soon as possible, keep your chin up! Bye for now!"

A few hours later a top level meeting was held aboard the Gravitas, with Heinrich and Judder invited as special guests.

Judder was the first to speak. "I bet that the mule had a cousin and he has sprung Trueblood from prison and has tried to take over the world again!"

The Whistler joined in with "That may actually be true because there was a cousin and a brother, but at the trials there was absolutely no evidence against them and they were discharged."

"Ok Judder, I think you have second guessed our possible solution and that is to use the Freeloader to smuggle all of the undercrews back down to earth. Or down to mars or some could be placed on the moon complex, we will explain the situation to them and give them a free choice of destination." Three weeks later the three ships only had skeleton crews and some of those were staying aboard to keep the ships functional. Two more lunar orbits were conducted and it was a relief to Eric and Kingdom that both their wives and families were alright. Judder's initial comments were proving to be very close to the mark. It *was* a cousin of the mule who was at the head of earth's government and Trueblood was heading the witch hunt for remaining Space personnel. He had approached Catherine Whistler and she had claimed to just be a clerk. Trueblood's arrogance was such that he took her at her word and crossed her off the surveillance list. This strange trait in his character gave the spacemen a route back down to earth. Catherine Whistler's house was situated in quiet countryside close to an aerospace museum, so no officials noticed when a couple of extra Space shuttles appeared, in the area left for unrestored examples of various craft. The noise made by the rocket engines was also lost during a violent thunderstorm. They were lucky.

Captain Johnson called a meeting using an empty hangar. He gave those folk around him a dire warning. "If Trueblood is out of prison, it is almost certain that the Prof is in. The powers that be will have our homes under surveillance. We have been lucky that no one has picked up our mobile phone links, so we must move carefully. Having said that, he suddenly started, as his mobile throbbed in his pocket. He fetched it out and pressed to accept the call.

"Kingdom, if that is you, just tap your phone twice in the approved manner!" Captain Johnson looked perplexed for a moment then remembered the coding given to Helen all those years ago. He fetched two coins out of his pocket and clacked them together.

The caller then rang off, but seconds later there was another gentle throb on the phone as it took a text message. He texted a reply and then waited expectantly. A small side door had opened and closed. Nobody heard or saw anything but the cold draught gave it away.

The widely grinning face of the Prof appeared from behind a column of palettes stood over at one corner. He had his finger across his lips commanding silence. He beckoned them over. Lifting a drain cover from the concrete floor he motioned the others to go down the steps revealed, he pulled the lid down after himself as he followed and shot a fastening bolt across on the underneath.

"God almighty Prof, what on earth has been going on?" said Captain Johnson.

"Firstly let me say that the authorities think I am dead and they are not looking for me!" he said. "They are however looking for Brian Judd and have been ever since he managed a mobile link from lunar orbit. Don't worry I have already had him intercepted and he is now with Nadine and their children hiding amongst my runner beans, or maybe in my loft, whichever they felt more comfortable with. There is food aplenty and so they have no direct need to chance shopping expeditions, or the like. Not too far from here is the Whistler's place, that is to say Eric's place, and Catherine is entertaining the complete Johnson brood. There is adequate space there and they know you are all in good health.

Trueblood scratched them from his surveillance list when Catherine told him she was just a filing clerk.

"She told him the truth there" protested Eric.

"Aye, she told him no lies, but Trueblood does not know of the Space Adventure book and who wrote it and just how much classified stuff comes her way. Nevertheless I do not want any clue of the whole truth to reach the Donkey's ears, and so I must impress on you the utmost care in conduct of your business. I dare say it will soon be common knowledge that you used the Freeloader to ship all those crew members back to earth, but I have started a rumour that the rest of you perished on final surreptitious descent in the shuttles that came down. I managed to use my army of contacts to fake re-entry burn out simultaneously hiding your successful re-entry today. I want you to plug this memory stick into the shuttle computors before we leave here today so any nosey parker will have information that the shuttles were on a pre-programmed earth return mission. Trueblood knows this is possible; he has had first hand experience of it!" he looked around the room.

"Christ, prof you have been busy!!!" exclaimed Henrik.

"Righty-ho" said the Prof "follow me back to you're shuttles, and we will put the memory sticks in and transfer the data. When you have done that plug these other memory sticks in and leave them.

"This leaves the Johnsons and the Whistlers taken care of, but what of my darling Helen and our son?" queried Henrik soberly.

She was in Nadine's loft with your little one up until about an hour ago, and she should be with us shortly!" smiled the Prof.

"Prof, are you Head of the resistance or something?" enquired Eric Whistler.

"I suppose I am but I am hoping to hand that job over to some one else shortly!" replied the Prof.

"Who would that be?" asked Captain Johnson, and pursed his lips thoughtfully as he realised all eyes were on him. "Prof, we are all tired, how quickly can we get ourselves to bed?" he asked.

"If you would all don these netting camouflage kits and follow me, we will see what is to be done", smiled the Prof, turning on his heel as soon as every one was ready. Captain Johnson realised that the Prof had a slight spring in his step and thought what sort of man was it that could gain energy from very adverse situations. "A bloody good one" he thought irreverently.

The captain was slightly miffed that Judder had escaped from their presence without him actually noticing and thanked god for the timely intervention of the Prof.

Five minutes later they had retrieved some small arms from the shuttles, and had plugged the programmed memory sticks in and then replaced them with ones that merely had a modern computor game on them. The rag-tag bunch, for that is what they were followed the Prof and climbed into a brand new van. "Hired you see, but with deliberately confusing hire data," smirked the Prof.

Half an hour later the Prof dropped them off and joined them and waited as some other resistance guy drove the van away.

"Follow me!!!" he walked carefully along until he came to a storm drain outlet and undid the latch on the lid. "There is a little truck inside there, last man, re-fasten the grid, me first I will send the truck back in a moment." Moments later the truck was back and Eric Whistler eased himself chest down exactly as the Prof had, and pulled him self along by means of a rope attached to the wall. The truck suddenly stopped with a bone jarring thud, and Eric could see a small amount of light above him. "Kick the truck back" hissed the Prof. Eric climbed up and out into a room that was almost in darkness, shortly the whole party was assembled there. "Last man, did you secure the entrance grid?" "Yes" came the reply. The Prof then pulled a small rope up and that moved the truck a little further along and lifted a round concrete disc up that effectively blocked the tunnel just after the vertical pipe. "That pipe will now return to its normal use of waste disposal from this building!" the Prof went to the windows and closed the venetian blinds and then put the lights on. He closed the floor access point and rolled the floor covering back over it.

"God almighty, it's the utility room at home gasped Eric Whistler.

"I have impressed upon every one the need for silence, so get up to bed and we will all talk in the morning." Urged the Prof. He pointed each man to his assigned room and then went in the end room himself and spent the rest of the night fretting over whether or not they had been detected.

There was some silent passion that night.

CHAPTER 20

WHAT ON EARTH DO WE DO NOW?

No-one was up much before noon, and the Prof had thoughtfully arranged for the children to be away with other relatives, on the pretext of giving the moms a little relief.

Henrik and Helen were last down, Helen looking a lovely guilty pink.

After taking a good breakfast, some talk began.

"I accept being head of the resistance" said Captain Johnson.

"Thank god for that, the job was wearing me out!" sighed the Prof.

Captain Johnson observed "following last nights little escapade I can understand why, but I did notice a somewhat jaunty spring in your step, you know!"

The Prof ignored this complement but said "It's a good job Helen inherited some of your shrewdness because somehow, she felt the bad vibes coming long before the war started and she moved all of the funds to a safe place. Because of that she is public enemy number one.

There is a massive underswell of opinion that wishes to see something akin to the old order back in place, but there is no cohesive movement. The minority government has a position where it is the only force with united purpose.

During the early months of the problems they murdered almost every Imam and Roman Catholic priest and this turned the whole world against the Protestants, until a huge swathe of them went for the chop as well. Too late the world realised just what it had unleashed against itself.

The new order wishes to control all of the money in the world. Amazingly they have left the Swiss banking system alone, and so the Space admin money is safe. They don't like it though!

Almost all of the workers of the Space administration have simply been starved of wages and so that organisation has simply fizzled away. Helen has records and if the world ever wakes up to itself, then she will make good their monies. However that will do no good if you starve to death in the meanwhile."

"Right, we need to move fast" ground Captain Johnson. "They don't think that any of us men are still alive do they? and that gives us a once only advantage.

I remember you flat footing the mule before, claiming to have invented teleporting. Wouldn't it be great if we could flat foot the Donkey in the same way? What if we can assemble a team of robotics engineers to fake a teleporting cabinet, and use magician's tricks to get people in and out? Create a climate of fear using a mob and persuade the Donkey to escape by the most elegant means known to man. In fact he would fall through the floor and be ground up for dog meat in a milling machine situated down below."

We would need a number of twins to participate and we could show them at home disappearing in a smoke filled cabinet and reappearing in another smoke filled cabinet some where else. One twin in, and the other twin out, so to speak.

We are in England just now, where does the Donkey reside?"

"That is difficult to say because he always appears on TV in some sort of neutral transmitting complex that could be anywhere, but I suppose he must be somewhere and we must track him down quietly causing no trouble. We could use a little led giving out UV rays, something not noticeable except to our detectors. We are well advanced enough to do that."

"Right, well that is a start. I suspect he will have put himself in the Pentagon or something similar. Now we need a number of gifted design engineers. There must still be a host of them in the US. And if we were to situate our development lab in say Canada or Alaska, then replacing someone who doesn't measure up should be easier. What about Japanese engineers?"

"Well ok" said the Prof, "I understand from news just breaking that a vast number of Shinto shrines have been destroyed and there are unconfirmed reports of many deaths over there. The Chinese and Indian governments have not yet capitulated to the Donkey, and they are so strong I really don't think the Donkey wants to take them on. He will close down various trade links and wait for the internal rebellions to begin before making his first move.

By the way, where is James?"

Captain Johnson was on his feet in a flash and he sprinted up the stairs and he burst into the room assigned to the Whistler. James Whistler was grey and sweating. "I was ok until I tried to take a glass of water this morning" he croaked.

Captain Johnson had seen this before. He rushed out and grabbed a bottle of Martian elixir and poured a little down the Whistler's throat, then gave him three anti-histamine capsules to swallow. 10 minutes later he began to revive, and the beads of sweat on his forehead slowly diminished.

"I thought I had had it, I could barely breathe" spluttered the Whistler.

"This is now personal" ground out Captain Johnson and the sound of his teeth crunching into each other could clearly be heard. This is Trueblood's doing, he left a contaminated glass of water just in case Catherine had fooled him. I have changed my mind. We don't need fancy cabinets or magic tricks, what we need are marksmen, we need poisoners, we need assassins of any sort, we need fire bugs we need lethal injection experts, and only the most determined of men will do!"

The moment we know where he is we will simply eliminate him. This is no time for lawful behaviour; we do not have the time. We also need to frighten him and we should eliminate Trueblood without delay. We need a list of his top henchmen, and we must eliminate as many of them as is possible in the shortest time.

Find a list of those who were tried and punished for association with the mule and we will warn all of them of their imminent death over the e- mail. Use internet cafes."

The meeting then involved others; Henrik was holding his blond son and gazing with fatherly tenderness at him as Helen looked on.

"Henrik could well be the prime target for the Donkey if the Donkey gets to hear that he is still alive," mused Captain Johnson, after all it was he that shot the Mule.

"Catherine," he asked "how well do you think you fooled Trueblood?"

"Reasonably" she said "but I wouldn't have if he had spotted Helen in the garden!"

Captain Johnson took a sharp intake of breath, "that was close" he stated the obvious, "I must formulate a plan to rid the earth of this scourge, so I need to know all of his possible whereabouts. Prof, would you please instruct me on the extent and operations of the underground please?"

"Gladly!" the Prof spoke for over an hour repeating the more important points. After this Captain Johnson's face was set grimly as he thought about how to get rid of the Donkey. He would need both carrot and stick; he would need total secrecy, so a lone assassin would be most likely to succeed. He knew that people like the Donkey were well versed in the use of modern technology, and that his TV appearances were always with the new holographic TV systems. The only reason for this would be to stay physically away from public places. The germ of an idea occurred to him.

"Prof, can we find out where all of the holographic transmitters and studios are, and can we arrange for a momentary transmission break from each one in turn?"

"Ah! Yes, I think our lads can do that. I see what you want, you want a programme of transmission breaks at specific times, so the instant his picture distorts, we will know which station he is being beamed from. Leave that to me, it will be done!"

CHAPTER 21

HOW CAN WE TRAP THE DONKEY?

Captain Johnson considered how this might be done. He instructed each of his inner group to carry a side arm. He told them to shoot first and ask questions afterwards.

He took Henrik to one side and said "Henrik you would replace Helen as public enemy number one if the Donkey knew you were alive. I have not formulated my plans yet, but I think you may be the carrot I am looking for to tempt this man out of hiding. I am presuming that the Donkey will be so consumed by hatred of you that he would want to dispose of you himself. I already know of your courage, but I must tell you that if you do as I suggest, you would be in immediate and continuous personal danger. I think the danger is so great I will not order you to do what I would like!"

"Captain, even Kingdom if I may be so bold; this Mule-Donkey dynasty must be destroyed or the world will regress thousands of years. I am mindful as well that we have a vulnerable colony on Mars and a handful of folk left on Stellar 2, if I can call it that. We must do something, and I have dreamt that I would somehow be in the vanguard again. May I make a suggestion?"

"Go ahead!"

"I heard from Helen just how you guarded her by confusing the spies, hiding her openly but in a group. That was a clever ruse and I wonder if we could do something similar. Imagine if I was in a holographic transmitting station but that my image was multiplied say 10 fold, so that there would be 10 of me. The transmissions could be done on low power so that they would only reach a range of say five miles where we could record the transmission.

I would issue a threat of death against the Donkey and brag that his cousin the mule was just as big an ass as he is and that I would get him and his team of murdering rats one at a time. He had better sleep with one eye open as we already have our spies planted in his organisation, and his days were numbered! We could send our recorded programme titled as, say, washing up liquid advert and it could be broadcast from every transmitter in the country during an advert slot and so would be untraceable. Come to think of it I could announce that the transmission was from orbit around Venus, so he wouldn't think I was down here in person!"

"Henrik that will require some polish to make it into a plan, but it is the best yet, better than any of my own ideas. I will ask the Prof about the practicalities of the recording and see if it could be done. Keep the idea under your hat for the moment and please don't tell Helen!"

Two days later the Prof appeared with one of the top holographic transmission engineers. The Prof then removed the blindfold, and the engineer looked nervously around at the men who all wore balaclava style hoods.

"I haven't broken any rules, and I have a wife and children to support," he almost begged.

"We are the resistance not the Donkey and his ass soldiers," boomed out one voice.

Ted Kowalski was not convinced. He thought that he was staring death in the face and was rather pale. "You are trying to entrap me, and get me to say something against the Donkey!" he wailed, but suddenly he stiffened as he realised death had come for him, and said "I would kill the bastard if I could!"

"Good man!" said one of the hooded group. "We will not ask you to do that, but we are going to ask you to help us to do it."

Ted Kowalski stared into Space and said "Bugger the lot of you. You might kill me but there are thousands of others who will take my place!"

The booming voice then rang out again "the pillock really thinks we are going to do away with him. We are hatching a plan and we desperately need some technical help. Sorry about the blindfolds and masks, but the less you know, the less danger you are in."

Ted thought desperately and said, "The whole of right thinking earth was awaiting the return of Captain Johnson and his colleagues as a focus for our dissatisfaction but they were all fried up on re-entry to earth, so now we are lost. Every so often, when a man's back is against the wall, he will fight because he has no option but to do that. I am that man, so do what you must with me, I am ready!"

Another voice spoke out and before the first part sentence was out Ted Kowalski swivelled his gaze around and drew a breath as he recognised Eric Whistler's voice.

"My god you didn't all fry on re-entry!" he gasped

"The less you know the better!" said another voice that he did not recognise, "but we *are* the resistance and you are in no danger from us. We wish to know if you could transmit a holographic image digitally split so that it would appear that there were say ten men, not one. We wish to record a message wherein the real man would issue death threats against the Donkey and his top aids. We wish to disguise the recording as an advert for some household item, bleach or washing powder for example, so that it could be transmitted at prime time and the first anyone would know of it was when the transmission was in progress. We need to anonymise it so that no one gets the blame for accepting the transmission. Can it be done?"

"Coffee!" demanded Ted Kowalski finally relaxing. "Keep your masks on, you are right, I need to know nothing, but I know how to start a rumour! I can say that I overheard some idiot farmer in the next room in a pub who actually believed that not all of the Space mission leaders were fried on re-entry. Intelligent people will embellish on that and before you know it there will be an army of resistance guys about to land from the big mission ships! Now with regard to your transmission idea I will need some time. Can you please steal my wallet so I have some story to tell with regard to my absence from home this evening?"

"We will keep it safe for you so please put on your mask and we will be in touch!"

Ted Kowalski was not the bravest of men and he had been surprised at how he had defied the Donkey as he had believed at the time. He felt in a better frame of mind than he had for months.

Before going home that night he called into his local police station and complained that he had been robbed at knifepoint by two masked men. The duty sergeant duly recorded his complaint and said it was probably the resistance guys looking for a bit of easy money. Ted used the station public phone to cancel his credit card and debit card.

That night his wife was puzzled by his general demeanour. He could not help but be upbeat. She said "you are the only man I know who would be happy having just been robbed!"

"I suddenly realised that things can't get much worse for a law abiding citizen like me, so they are bound to get better, and it was as if a huge load was lifted from my shoulders."

Sheila looked at him shrewdly and thought "the old bugger is up to something," but she couldn't imagine what it might be.

CHAPTER 22

THIS WASN'T GOING TO BE EASY

Ted Kowalski put on his thinking cap. He tried to keep his idea simple. How could he simply transmit an advert without some-one knowing the source of the recording? He considered how he might bluff his way through. Mostly adverts went out at the same time over several regions simultaneously, and this involved precision timing. Most times this went without a hitch, but on occasions, if a transmission was delayed, the adverts came in on schedule and the end few seconds of a programme simply disappeared, this usually occurred when the music was playing and the cast of characters was rolling, so no harm done and very few viewer complaints. The studio clocks were all synchronised to either summer time or winter time. Shortly on the last Sunday in October the clocks would all go back one hour.

He pondered this issue. The clocks all went back at 2 am so as to inconvenience the fewest people.

If he was to arrange the rogue transmission at that time in the morning, everybody including him would be at home asleep in bed. Furthermore very few viewers would still be up to see it. But there would be a few and good healthy rumours could grow out of it. He had already mentioned the mystery farmer in a pub who believed that some of the Space mission adventurers had not suffered re-entry burn up. He had been cunning doing this. He was not speaking to anyone at the time but he spoke so that the guy at the next table who sat back to back with him could catch some of the words.

He was gratified as he went out when he overheard the rumour being repeated, so he knew that it would be difficult to track down the originator, as the guy who had been his target had already repeated it to as many people as would listen; now for the nitty gritty. He rang around some of his colleagues in the commercial section and asked what the quickest way to formulate an advert was, and in particular how much it would cost.

One chap was quite helpful "the cost will depend on the length of the ad and the time of transmission! If you had a twenty second ad transmitted at 0200 hours, the costs would be a fraction of the costs for a one minute ad at prime time."

Ted said, "But the only adverts at that time of the day are for dating sites and the like, so who the hell would watch them?"

His contact gave him the telephone number of the night time programme controller and suggested he asked again.

Again Ted put his thinking cap on, and then rang the controller, explaining that he had been approached to simply find out how adverts were vetted etc and then how to go about getting a transmission.

The programme controller sighed. "Look there are very strict rules, and if you are caught taking a kick-back you could lose your job!"

Ted sounding suitably awed, adding, "No its nothing like that its just that I was at a party and this guy wants to get into the dating agency business and he knows he is going to have to get an ad on the telly to get his business up and running and he thought I might know how best to go about it, well I didn't, but I am a little more informed now. How do you go about getting your advert vetted?"

"Make up a disc and send it to the Programme Controllers Dept for us to see and then we will tell them the result within a couple of days!"

Ted's idea was now complete, and he needed to talk to the resistance. He left work early and went into his local pub. It was a cool day and he remarked to the landlord that he wished he had got a balaclava. He drank his pint and walked outside to the car park and smiled as he felt the hood slip over his head and he followed the pressure on his arm. Half an hour later he was sat down and the hood was removed.

"You have an idea Ted?"

"Indeed I do. It has diverged somewhat from the notion that you gave me, but I think it should do exactly what you want.

Firstly you must open up a website and make sure that your message is on that website. I dare say you could use an internet café.

You must watch a bit of late night telly and wait for the dating adverts to come on. Then you must make an advert very similar to one of them. These adverts usually have a text or phone number for the viewer to ring, but in your case these will be false numbers. Also on there will be the website address. This advert will go out at about two in the morning so it won't be seen by many people. There is bound to be some randy sod that will go on line to check the website out. Maybe several hundred depending on how sexy the girls on the dating site advert appear. Perhaps you could get the advert disc to contain a second website address where perhaps an E or an I, have been interchanged so that the first time that it is run it will display the correct address but after that only the E, I, changed address. The Donkey's men will get to hear about this transmission and they will rush to the studio to confiscate the disc, while they examine it. Your men must attack and kill some of the Donkey's men but let one escape so that the Donkey thinks his men have done a good job. It may take them anything from a few minutes to a few hours to unravel the mystery and in the meantime you can put a second message on if that will help. Your anonymity should be well preserved and there is nothing like a good rumour to get under the skin of these all powerful murderers that are running things just now. I have started the rumour that there are survivors from the fry up already!" He told them of his efforts in that regard, and asked if they approved his idea.

One of the hoodies laughed out loud. "That is about as good as it gets!"

"Where do we get the women from?" came a voice from the back.

Ted added that he thought the local theatricals, the 'luvvies' as he called them may well be up for a few easy shekels.

"Thank you Ted, hood on please!" within forty minutes ted was back at the pub but they drove him to the next pub before de-hooding him.

He was just going to say that it was the wrong pub when he spotted his own car, grinned at his captors as he went off.

He walked in a bout forty minutes late and Sheila looked at him expectantly. "You've been up the pub!" she scolded.

He admitted that he had. "I have been after a bit of promotion but I don't think I will get it," he said.

"Ah I knew you were up to something" she said and largely believed him. She wasn't entirely fooled but could detect no sign of lipstick or perfume so she was satisfied that he wasn't playing away, and decided to let matters unfold as they may.

CHAPTER 23

THE RESISTANCE BOYS PLAY THEIR PART

About a week after the last meting with Ted Kowalski, rumours reached their ears that the re-entry burn up was a ruse put about by the Donkey because he was scared. This was even better if it reached the Donkey in that form as it would both infuriate and frighten him.

The internet café idea was expanded and about 10 different accounts were set up.

The younger women from the local repertory company swallowed that they were auditioning for a new role that was still top secret and they were inveigled into acting out a few moments as sexy sirens. The whole of the rest of the stuff was still going to be used on the nine bogus internet accounts, and they willingly played roles from Macbeth to Christmas pantomimes.

Henrik Svensson was a little disappointed to find he was only on an ordinary camcorder and not on holographic recordings but he made a good job of recording his chilling message which in its final form went: "Hello Donkey. Are you really that big an ass? We are all here and your life is drawing to a close. Your time is up. Never sleep without body guards if you think you can trust them. I shot your little fart of a cousin, and I will shoot you. Bye for now!"

The camcorder used was an old one and it gave the recording a slightly ghostly image. Though this was due to some setting error it was decided to leave it alone just for the effect.

Six days later the approved dating advert went out. The resistance used Ted Kowalski's credit card, as Ted had hoodwinked the station sergeant when he made the cancellation and in effect he Ted had been not been speaking to the credit card company but speaking to some unknown guy in the north of England who put the phone down when he had heard enough.

Nothing happened for about three days but then the TV studio got a bunch of heavies paying them a visit. They had tracked down where the disc had originated from. Ted Kowalski had no problem playing a terrified man. These hard nutters were not funny. Ted surrendered the disc unwillingly saying how it was more than his job was worth to give it to a third party. This remark caused one of the heavies to lay him out, and Ted went down like a glass chinned boxer.

The resistance fighters were waiting out side and a short but furious gunfight ensued. Only one heavy was spared and he rushed to one of his fallen comrades and fished the disc from his breast pocket before thanking his lucky stars as he made it to his landrover. Bullets followed the landrover as he gunned it away from the car park. Within five hours the Donkey played the disc and then tapped the website address but he got an advert for a Chinese restaurant in Mexico. He had heard description of the transmitted detail and knew that he was up against someone who was a worthy adversary, and used his ability for lateral thinking, which was appreciable; after several frustrating failures he cracked it, and then sat in chilled disbelief as Henrik Svensson appeared, exactly as he had on the TV. He felt a cold dagger of fear invade his inner being and he did not like it. He was used to others trembling before him!

He knew that there was a world wide rag bag of dissident resistance movements. They were rubbish he told himself, but he was an astute man and reasoned that Henrik Svensson could be like the pope was to the Roman Catholic religion. He was a focal point.

"I have to rid the world of him and then the resistance will crumble," he thought.

He remembered how easy it had been to use the badly disenchanted public to aid him in his election campaign. There was only a muted outcry when he sent the entire British government and the leaders of the opposition to the firing squad, and how almost to his surprise the news of this propagated through Europe and the United States with similar results. He had been the driving force then. He had been unstoppable.

Now the world really knew what he stood for and there was well over half of the populace ready to get rid of him. The thing was he held sway over the armies of the subjugated countries, and he similarly controlled the policing operation every where in the previously democratic countries except in Africa. In Africa there was such a proliferation of self interested factions that the whole place was in danger of destroying itself. There were many examples of genocide but the mule didn't care, he knew Africa would welcome him with open arms, as only he was ruthless enough to rid Africa of its self interested warlords. He knew as the trade which the developing world relied upon was stopped that even India and China would eventually crumble, though his personal desire for world domination did not include these latter two. He had left the Swiss banking system alone and had reinforced Swiss neutrality. After all when he retired he would need money and some where to go. He awoke from this reverie and called in his top aides, including professor Trueblood. He played the disc and hooked up to the website, so that every one had seen everything,

"Well gentlemen, ideas on first course of action. He turned first to Trueblood, who simply stood transfixed. "Professor, what am I paying you for!" he barked. Trueblood's mouth worked but very little sound came out. He was terrified.

The Donkey nodded to another of the top aids and he took Trueblood by the arm saying "canteen for you my boy!" Trueblood went willingly. A few minutes later the sound of a single shot rang out, and the Donkey said "I hope that will sharpen your wits, now what is to be done?"

Trueblood died with the unspoken question of why on his lips.

When the assassin got back to the inner chamber he nodded at the Donkey and then offered the following as soon as he had caught up with the conversation.

This man was sharp and in between bouts of coughing said. "We always knew there would be a resistance, and now they seem to have a leader. That guy Svensson lived in England so he would be able to marshal resources there, but we are a world wide organisation so I think we should offer you as bait and try to tempt them out of the woodwork. I think the holographic TV system can be used to give you a pseudo personal appearance and we will publish local news stating that you will be there in person. I am sure that this will precipitate attempts on your life and we will deal with anyone who even looks like he might be able to carry a gun.

If we can get a result now the embryo resistance will die before birth. Oh and when we catch Svensson I want first shot!"

The Donkey nodded as he considered the proposal, "Ok Fordy, agreed, perhaps you would like to get on with that, urgently of course."

Fordy, actually Donald Ford was the twin brother of Peter Ford who had almost been ejected into Space and therefore had good reason to hate the Space authorities. The Donkey was a cousin of the late Nick Jackson known as the Mule. He was Don Jackson, and had carried the nickname of the Donkey due to his clumsy efforts at football at school. It now seemed an appropriate nickname, as a follow on to the Mule. If anything he was more practical than his cousin had been and equally as clever. All in all he was a more dangerous man, and had continued recruiting for his organisation right through the days of the big trials held at the end of his cousin's era.

The only thing that the Donkey was as yet unaware of was the extent of the network of sympathisers enjoyed by the resistance.

The last act as leader of the resistance carried out by the Prof was to get small UV emitting mini-lamps installed all over the globe, inside the holographic transmission studios. The technicians fitting them were not all resistance fighters, but were simply following orders. The Morse like code given to each device was transmitted in the teletext bar which was out of sight and in fact out of use on all modern TV's. The Prof's TV had of course been adjusted to display the bar. He and a handful of followers watched the bars avidly each time there was a holographic transmission. They were pleased to find that each studio could be identified when it was the primary source of transmission. The TV designers had been clever and the signals used to generate a holographic transmission still played out on an ordinary digital TV so you could still watch the programme with an older TV.

News of professor Trueblood's demise got out, and the resistance immediately claimed to have killed him. This of course had no effect whatever on the Donkey and his circle of top aids, but it did sow seeds of doubt amongst the lower ranks, and gave rise to a mini surge of righteousness among the populace.

The Donkey would have to keep his best thinking hat on or else he would be outwitted. He knew this and relished the challenge.

CHAPTER 24

FORDY'S PLAN GOES INTO OPERATION

Advance word reached the ears of the public of a personal appearance of the Donkey.

Reports came in from various regions of the resistance that the public appearance would be in their region.

The resistance used their international contacts to spy on the goings on. Since Kingdom Johnson had assumed leadership of the resistance he had been able to establish connections with the resistance in the Americas. He had made contact with people who already new him but he got the Prof to do the talking so that no one as yet knew he was now the driving force.

The Donkey made his 'appearance' and the resistance were under strict orders to not mount any attempt on his life. A number of body guards were deployed at each of the so called personal appearance sites. The Prof watched the transmission bars and located ten different sites but none of them was the prime transmission site.

"It is almost like he copied Henrik's plan" he mused. Suddenly the Morse code lamp blinked again just as the transmission closed. The Prof looked up the code in his table and said, "Christ, the bugger is in Bristol!"

Back in the other camp, Fordy was surprised that no attempt on the Donkey's life had been made. The Donkey however wondered whether they had overestimated the strength of the resistance and reasoned that there had been insufficient time for the resistance to act upon information received.

"Well they are bound to have heard about your appearance now so I think we should wait a week and then repeat the exercise. After all I think your message to the people will have smoothed quite a number of worried brows."

The Prof meanwhile had talked things over with Judder and they had agreed to put all three of the British sites in Bristol, London and Edinburgh onto a red alert state. It was known that the Donkey had been in the Bristol studios and that cunningly he had not used any bodyguards. The resistance had kept a watch on every port and airport in the British Isles, and it was believed that the Donkey was still in the UK.

For the next transmission Fordy had persuaded the Donkey to surround himself with body guards, on the premise that he had got away with it once but after that it would mean taking unnecessary risks.

During the transmission it was detected that the Donkey was in the Edinburgh studios.

The local resistance was made up of a number of very dour men and they sprang into action covering every exit. One hour after the transmission had finished there was no sign of the Donkey and the local resistance leader realised that somehow he had been spirited away, but he gave orders to kill as many bodyguards as could be identified. This resulted in the deaths of seventeen men, four of whom were resistance fighters.

In fact the Donkey had only managed to exit the studio three or four minutes before, then the gunfire could plainly be heard, and he was shaken by this.

He had dressed in a black burkha and simply walked out to the car park and driven away.

The worm of fear had taken root in his inner being and would affect his reasoning and his judgement in the weeks to come.

Fordy thought that once again the Donkey had soothed people with his particular brand of rhetoric. The Donkey was not quite as intuitively skilled as his cousin had been, but he was a beautiful orator in his own right, though what Fordy had not taken into account was the sophistication of his audience. Far from having their brows soothed, the general public was irritated by the rhetoric which was plainly inaccurate.

The old political guard had got away with what used to be called 'spin,' and it was due to the continuous diet of spin drivel, that disenchantment amongst the electorate rose to the point where the electorate thought that anything must be better than this. They had been very wrong. It took perhaps two years before the level of malcontentedness reached the present day level.

The attempt on the Donkey's life had been sanitised before the press got anything to publish and according to the press release, a band of known dissidents had been simply overrun and killed several hours after the Donkey had left the area. Some people will believe anything but most were already tired of the way in which the Donkey's government conducted itself, even those who had no idea what the real truth was simply gave the Donkey no credit, and every incident such as the one described above whittled at the support that the Donkey had and gradually weakened his position.

The Prof and Judder with their instinctive grasp of the situation realised that headway could be made without killing the Donkey at this stage, and they applied themselves to the task of bringing about the downfall of this evil man.

Kingdom Johnson prepared an accurate bulletin, naming those killed in Edinburgh he extolled the virtue of the resistance fighters and castigated the others.

This news was broken via the internet in Mexico and Canada simultaneously. Radio hams world wide transmitted the details and before twenty four hours had passed this news was the subject of an urgent meeting in the inner sanctum of the Donkey.

All over the affected parts of the world there was a rising expectation that things were about to change.

The Donkey's response was typical; he sent henchmen out and despatched several broadcast journalists summarily. He made no effort to establish whether any of them were guilty and expected the fear engendered by his action to crush the hopes of the populace. He was so wrong.

He made another 'personal appearance' and even he could recognise that even if he told the truth, he would not be believed. He was very, very angry, and tried to take out his temper on his first lieutenant. He lambasted Fordy again and again. Fordy was no fool and he knew his own days were numbered. He made plans inside his own head to get rid of the Donkey, but he knew if he were to do that, his own life wouldn't be worth a plugged nickel. He would end up spread across a pub car park or the like.

The following day when the Donkey had cooled off somewhat he called another meeting. As the meeting progressed the worm of fear began once again to get the upper hand in his psyche. He suddenly accused Fordy of behaving like his brother and wasting opportunities. This meaningless accusation was based on zero fact, but it cut Fordy to the quick. He had the presence of mind to keep cool and wait for the meeting to end. As he went out he knew what his course of action was to be, and who he would have to contact.

CHAPTER 25

WHAT WAS THE RESISTANCE TO MAKE OF THIS?

The Donkey craved popularity and felt a failure when he knew that he would never be popular. This unfortunately elevated the cruel side of his nature to the point where his entire inner cabinet feared for their lives if they said one word out of place.

News came in to the resistance network of something unusual, and Judder was sent to investigate.

In a quiet pub in the north of England some guy had got drunk and had openly bragged that he knew how to kill the Donkey. Three days later the same man made the same claim in the same pub. Judder installed himself in the only hotel in the village and visited the pub to see for himself. There were only a handful of men in there but suddenly one of the locals got up and went to the bar, and ordered a pint of beer. While this was being drawn he fished coins out of his pocket and absently clacked two of them together. Judder clacked two pound coins, and then walked outside and waited and though he didn't smoke he lit a cigarette. A few moments later the coin clacker also exited the pub.

"The guy you want is sitting in the alcove over near the fireplace!" he then turned on his heel and went away into the night.

Judder walked back in and threw his dog end into the fire, then sat down and began to read a newspaper that was lying on the seat. Behind this he carefully got his mobile phone out and filmed the suspect. As the evening wore on the suspect began to sound more and more drunk, and though he was slurring his words he claimed that the world would be better off without the Donkey and he knew how to get rid of him.

The following day the phone film was downloaded onto the Prof's lap top and the photo control package on the computor successfully cleaned up the images.

`The film was shown to all of the Space Captains.

Eric Whistler nodded and said "He is just like Peter Ford, who I nearly ejected into Space. In fact he is so like him he must be his brother."

The assembly scanned such records as they had, and found just one news item when the Donkey had been making his play as other older governments fell prey to their own dishonesty. There close at hand was one Donald Ford, and they further researched him. They concluded that he was likely the number two in the Donkey's organisation.

The Prof advised caution, "Imagine for a moment that the Donkey wants to destroy us. What better way than to use a top official and plant him into our organisation!"

Eric Whistler volunteered to fetch the man in for questioning. "I will recognise him better than anyone else here, and if I take a team of hand picked men, we can snaffle him from the carpark take him to that hangar through the underground tunnels and we can give him a thorough grilling. We will pump him full of truth drugs and grill him again in the approved manner. Having done that we will try to frighten the life out of him then dump him back on the carpark and await results!"

This was duly done and Fordy gave them a list of real places where the Donkey would be. He also told the resistance that he hated the guts of the Space service and Eric Whistler in particular for ejecting his twin brother into Space without a fair trial.

A piece of paper was given to him which simply said "Peter Ford alive and well in jail on Titan.

Fordy looked and blinked and coughed his characteristic hack. "Pencil please!" and he wrote some unintelligible drivel on it, saying "he will know what I mean. Bring me his reply and I am your man!"

One of his hooded captors interjected "Watch the TV after midnight and look for your reply!"

Fordy was then re-hooded and bundled down the tunnel and into a waiting van in the back. After half an hour he was ejected from the van onto a grass verge about 100 yards from the pub.

A few nights later as he was watching his TV, Fordy was startled by a rapid flash on the screen which said "GRONTLEWICH". The transmission was so brief that he thought it was his imagination, but twenty minutes later right in the middle of an advert for forthcoming programmes the same word briefly flashed on. It was his nonsense character that he and his twin brother made up when they were little boys, whenever questioned by their parents over some wrongdoing, Grontlewich got the blame. He had believed the Donkey when he had been told that his twin brother had been ejected into Space as a traitor. At the time due entirely to this lie, he had refused to watch any of the televised trial proceedings. He realised now that the Donkey was shown up as a liar even to his closest associates. His hatred previously focused on the world in general and the Space administration in particular, now found its new focal point on his boss, the Donkey.

The following day he went to the pub, and the day after that, and the day after that. He was just beginning to doubt whether they would contact him again, when he was firmly hooded and bundled into the back of a large pantechnicon.

As this large vehicle bumped its way out of the country lanes and onto a better road a light came on and he found himself looking at half a dozen hooded men. Before any of them could speak he blurted out "My brother is alive, alive, alive! I have gone too far down the road with the Donkey to expect forgiveness, though up until recently I hadn't got any blood directly on my own hands, but I killed Trueblood."

"Listen, we cannot guarantee you immunity from prosecution when the world regains its rightful legal system, but it would bode well for you, and perhaps for your brother if you could help us get rid of the Donkey. Trueblood was a duplicitous self opinionated arrogant and murderous character. He was one of our prime targets and no-one here will mourn his passing. We have already decided that all normal laws are suspended until we can re-establish democracy, so don't spend too much time worrying about that!"

Fordy described to them what had been going on and how he knew that his own life would surely be forfeit if he stayed with the Donkey for much longer.

"What we need is to know where the Donkey is going to make his next appearance!"

Fordy sighed and said, "That may be difficult because he changes his mind literally at the last second, but I could give you his four choices. He usually has only four choices because the organising of trustworthy body guards becomes increasingly difficult with each additional venue, I will text you this as soon as I can but I will wipe the text from my phone as soon as it has been sent"

Captain Johnson who was at the back of the vehicle said suddenly, "Agreed but you will be watched!" he strode forward and gave Fordy the number to text to.

Fordy suddenly realised in spite of the hood, from whom he was taking the paper, and said, "The Donkey is already in a blue funk just knowing that Henrik Svensson is on his trail. If he knew you were still alive it would add to his woes."

"No-one burned up on re-entry!" came another voice from the back. Fordy did not recognise this voice but he had no doubt that what he had just heard was the plain truth.

At the back of his mind he thought that just maybe he could salvage redemption for himself and his twin brother.

Captain Johnson spoke again. "Democracy has so far proven the best form of government, but democracy starts at the top, not at the bottom. Governments around the world including the British and American governments have had too many officials, who considered themselves to be from 'the ruling class,' and how somehow the notions of democracy, honesty and decency were not for them. These people were dangerous and will be weeded out and punished heavily. We must ensure that never again can they become so infatuated with their own importance that they stop thinking about others further down the scale, thus paving the way for the likes of the Donkey. What we wish to do is to re-establish the rule of law, but the courts would be loaded with a new task. They and they alone would decide upon any punishment of guilty parties according to an agreed scale, and the judiciary will not be known to the public. There would be no interference from the political powers or any other power on pain of death. A separate judicial watch dog would be set up and this organisation would be checked for legal operation by the judiciary but would have power of life or death over the judiciary, and would be expected to provide an annual assessment of the performance of the judiciary. In effect each branch would have massive power over the other and thus the two would have to stay straight just to survive. Any sign of collusion from one to the other would be punishable by life imprisonment. The prime function of the judiciary would be to act in a manner commensurate with seeing that justice is both done and seen to be done. No member of the judiciary would be able to hide behind some obscure law to protect himself, or take the easy way out when difficult decisions had to be made, he would be expected to set a precedent but would be aware at that time that his decisions would be scrutinised carefully.

Free speech will once again be to the fore, but people who abused that privilege must face the consequences of their own words, the law will not give them personal protection. However as a back up to this to encourage responsible free speech, the death penalty option will be re-introduced. There will be no such thing as a political crime. You are either guilty of something or not. Motives will only be considered when considering the length of any sentence but that is all. Drugs such as cannabis will be allowed for medicinal purposes. Any one caught distributing or in any way propagating the drug culture will face a suspended sentence—on the end of a rope.

I have told you all this Mr Ford because we need an inside man, and I have detected in you a spark of decency which has not hitherto been allowed to flourish.

Openness and honesty is the armour plating against the mouths of those who wish to bring discredit on others. We wish to restore democracy, but back to the real democracy. We think the world will agree, and we believe that a five year healing plan will be needed to place a salve on the festering wounds left by the Donkey. It may be that when the resistance is dissolved the first civilian government will be an interim one, and will have some of the resistance people in it. The various religious factions around the world will be free to practice their religion, but there will only be one law in each country, and it will be an offence to try to introduce another legal system except through the ballot box, where every voter will have a say. On matters of great import the referendum system will be applied.

One of our number is an Englishman, and he has told me of a comedy programme that used to be on British TV. We are adopting the programme title as our slogan. The title is "Drop the dead Donkey."

Fordy started to laugh but was overtaken by his hacking cough.

Another hooded voice then spoke up, "It sounds to me as if you need some-one to look at your health, and though many a casket of ashes wishes it could cough like that, it would be better cured, I think. It is Friday night and I believe that you are still a bachelor, with no family ties. If that is so then I suggest that you are examined within the hour!"

Fordy suddenly relaxed and thanked them as in truth he had wanted to see a doctor for some time, and he confessed "I would like that. It would be the end of me if the Donkey found out I was ill, so I just hoped it would get better on its own. It hasn't. I know that it is my position inside the Donkey Empire that interests you, and not my salvation but I must say that in your speech a few moments ago you addressed many of the issues festering inside me and my brother and I hope you can deliver. I fear that may not be so easy. The Donkey expressed many similar sentiments to me early in his reign but as time has progressed he has fallen further and further away from the promises that he made.

My brother and I have both backed wrong horses haven't we?"

Within an hour he was seen by a top lung specialist and taken covered with a blanket like a criminal entering or leaving a court.

Fordy was lucky, there was no underlying serious issue, and he was given a sizeable bottle of some linctus.

The boys in the resistance were not yet to know, but Captain Johnson's little impromptu speech had turned Fordy. He was now truly their man. He would accept the insults from the Donkey and just work quietly at providing information about the goings on via the text message service.

CHAPTER 26

FORDY SEES SOME CHANGES

From time to time he would visit the pub, and every so often he would be grabbed. He always marvelled at this because the stealth and speed of the resistance men was such that even if he wasn't willing to go, he had no chance to put up a fight.

On this particular night about six weeks from his allegiance change, he had some interesting news for them. The Donkey had heard from his American branch that the Space mission commanders had not been burned up. This was not due anyone letting the resistance down, but due to a young engineer who had been studying some data given as part of a university project. The young lady was not to know that the data was that showing the re-entry of the Space mission crew. She spotted an anomaly and using her considerable powers of deduction had realised that something did not quite add up. After wrestling with this for a while she concluded that the data had deliberately been falsified by persons unknown and that the ships successfully landed somewhere in Europe possibly in England.

She handed the work in to her mentor and he was suitably impressed and found that he agreed with her logic. Word of this little discovery broke and came to the ears of the Donkey's men. Within the hour the Donkey knew. He had called a meeting and Fordy was in on the meeting.

The Donkey far from looking more worried as one may have expected, actually looked relieved. "At last I know why things have been difficult for the last few weeks" he said. The resistance is using the leadership skills of the Space missioners. Fordy I want you to find out just what is going on, and I don't want to see you again until you have information!"

"I would have to go underground," said Fordy carefully, "I don't think my face is generally known so I will have to start some rumours and wait for some-one to grab me. I could be away for several days provided they don't suss out who I am."

"You have a fortnight at the outside" the Donkey grudgingly conceded. "I suppose that there really is no other way. After a fortnight I will consider that you have failed and I will replace you, though I must say your cough seems better. As a matter of fact I almost replaced you three weeks ago because of that cough. As you know I insist on my executives all being in perfect health."

Fordy realised he had been even closer to his demise than he had hitherto believed and was glad that the opportunity had fallen so neatly to him to contact the resistance. "I will never let you down!" he said briskly, and the Donkey nodded curtly at him.

Fordy stood and gathered his notes. "Where are you going?" questioned the Donkey.

"Unless I am mistaken my fortnight is already a few minutes old!" he replied. As he left the room he just caught the Donkey extolling the virtue of a man such as Don Ford.

He smiled inwardly and managed to suppress the cough that wanted to get out. He put on his coat and went to the pub. He hadn't even got inside when he sensed a presence close at hand.

"Not this pub, find me another pub!" he hissed. He saw and heard nothing and had just begun to think he had imagined it when he felt a hand in his pocket. He froze and the hand withdrew. He went into the pub had a pint and then went to the toilet. There was a scrap of paper with another pub marked on it. He new the pub and it was on the other side of the village; he left the toilet fastened his coat around him and adjusted his scarf. He reached into his pocket and fetched the paper out then screwed it up into a ball and flicked it onto the fire. It flared up immediately.

He made his way to the second pub and as he locked his car, his stomach flickered as the hood covered his head. This time when the hood was removed he found himself with only three jailers.

"The Donkey knows that there was no re-entry fry-up" he said and he described how the secret had been broken. "I must say that I thought the Donkey would be in a panic, but he is not. He appeared to be relieved and he has charged me with finding out what is going on. He has agreed that I should go underground, so here I am, and he has allowed me a fortnight."

"Fordy, I believe that the Donkey has outguessed us, and he has set you up. If you go back now it will be to certain execution. Imagine for sake of argument that he suspected you. He has found a way of getting rid of you for a fortnight, and he will check progress. Over the coming fortnight he will consider the problems and if the nature of his problems changes he will blame you no matter how they change. He is a clever lad you know."

Fordy reached into his pocket and offered a disc to his captors. "That at the time of my leaving was the itinerary he planned for the next few days. If he does not follow that itinerary then I fear you are correct, and I must say that he changes such things at a moments notice. I know his logistics chaps get very little sleep."

Fordy thought for a moment. "If you order me to go back I will go back. But I must admit that I don't want to. I have considered what Captain Johnson said the other night and I believe every word. I have realigned my allegiance and I am no longer the butt of the Donkey's bad humour. I wish to be part of the resistance. The thing that changed me was the truth about my brother. I realise that the Donkey would use threats against my brother to control me, whereas you will not and all in all I awoke the morning after our last contact with a different outlook. You must be cautious, so I expect nothing in the short term. Thank you for your medical help, I do feel quite a bit better now. Just in case you are wondering, I recognised Captain Johnson's voice. So I know it was him."

The three men simultaneously pulled off their masks. Fordy blinked but did not recognise two of them. The first man stepped forward and said "Brian Judd better known these days as Judder!"

The second followed suit saying "Henrik Svensson!"

The third came forward and in his rather scholarly way said "Doctor Barry!"

Henrik Svensson then said, "I found myself caught up in the mule's entourage, so I do know what it is like to be on the wrong side."

Fordy smiled and said "yes but you never really changed your allegiance. I have done that twice now, firstly when I threw my lot in with the Donkey, and just the other night when I got off his back and climbed onto another horse, if that is not too strong a pun. It is not easy to change allegiance and I do feel a bit like a soldier of fortune, but Captain Johnson spoke in such a way as to provide me with a jigsaw piece that fits exactly into the hole in my mind. I was brassed off with the various governments around the world none of whom ever said anything straight and simple and I believed that the Donkey was the answer. Well believe me I now know that he really isn't."

Right at that moment the staccato bang of gunfire was plainly heard and the vehicle they were in swerved violently then came to a screeching halt.

"Christ he has had me followed" said Fordy. "He will attack from three sides so that none of his own men will be caught in their own crossfire, the men will be deployed dead ahead and at one twenty degrees in a circle round the van." A trap door over the vehicle prop shaft was lifted by Doctor Barry and he unstrapped a spare wheel from the side of the vehicle and looked at the puncture marks in it. "There are certainly men dead ahead" he confirmed. He pushed the wheel down through the trap exit and then followed it down. All four men then lay beneath the vehicle. Doctor Barry positioned the spare wheel to protect them from dead ahead and guessed that the rear wheels should give some protection from the crossfire as gunfire erupted once again. This confirmed Fordy's claim as to the disposition of their attackers.

Fordy suddenly wriggled over to the grass verge then disappeared into the trees. "We shall soon know about his allegiance now," whispered Doctor Barry.

Fordy went through the trees as if to the manor born he was as silent as he could be and soon came to the group on the left side of the road behind the resistance fighters. He used his military training to make an assessment, and used a stick from the ground as he poked the youngest looking of the assassins in the back of the neck. "Freeze!" he whispered. The young soldier froze and never felt the removal of his AK47. He knew he was in trouble when he finally turned round to look behind him. There was no sign of anyone there.

The characteristic sound of an AK47 erupted, as it used about half its ammunition. There were some muted cries and then silence for several minutes.

Fordy suddenly whispered to his resistance colleagues, "wriggle over here, I've got weapons!"

Within seconds Henrik Svensson held an AK47. He had never held one before but this device had been a favourite amongst soldiers ever since it was invented about a century before. Fordy ordered the others to stay low and he melted into the darkness again. The bark of the AK47 rent the night once again, then silence. Henrik Svensson suddenly wriggled forward and went along the verge of the road, and was rewarded when he saw a number of men suddenly stand and begin moving towards their truck, as they did so the AK47 opened up again and as the soldiers all turned to face their unseen enemy, Henrik Svensson let rip. The AK47 tried to leap from his grasp, but he held on to it and then got in a second burst. The two pronged attack surprised the remaining Donkey's men but they rallied and turned to face Henrik Svensson. He was out of ammunition and flung himself flat down just as another AK47 opened up and cut into the donkeys men. One man threw his weapon down and began raising his arms but unfortunately he had a destiny with a bullet already on its way and he went down as though poleaxed.

Fordy realised that the skirmish was over and ran full pelt back to the van. The driver was shakily stepping down from the cab as Fordy got there, with blood seeping from a shoulder wound, but was otherwise ok.

Fordy grinned as the others got back and said "Well how did I do?" before they could reply however he grabbed an AK47 and rushed across into the woods. The original lad that he had disarmed was still there, basically quaking in his boots. Fordy grinned at the lad and told him to "piss off!" but his ears had caught the sound of a wounded man groaning. "Wait, you can help me get this man to a doctor!" he said. Fordy and the lad carried the injured man and dumped him by the local phone box. "Is the van still driveable?" he yelled. It was and so Fordy rang for the ambulance and left the shaken young lad and the injured man to be collected. Half an hour later the resistance group were at one of their safe houses and cups of tea were handed round. Fordy had sustained a wound on top of his one thigh. It was only a graze but he was presented with a clean towel and some sticking plasters and went to clean himself up. He was humming as he came back.

"Account for your attitude!" demanded Henrik Svensson.

"For the first time in a long time I know I was on the right side and I am proud of myself!" said Fordy a little defensively.

"Good, well get this down you!" grinned Henrik offering a slug of Irish whiskey.

Fordy smiled as he realised that he was now accepted and swallowed the whiskey. It brought on a sudden bout of coughing.

Doctor Barry chimed in with "I think we shall need to add cough mixture to our emergency supplies cabinet!"

Henrik Svensson said "right ho, initial debriefing. I ran to help Fordy but my AK47 ran out of ammo probably because it was already half empty, but someone else saved my bacon, who was it?"

"It was me that gave the final fusillade just as they were about to give up," admitted Doctor Barry. "I still thought they looked determined and I knew Fordy would be low on ammo so I just let them have it!"

"That is how I got my flesh wound!" said Fordy philosophically, but I had still got this AK47 with a full magazine," he held the weapon up.

Doctor Barry then realised that some of his bullets had gone past his intended target and apologised to Fordy profusely.

Fordy nodded acknowledgment to doctor Barry then spoke again "Judder, I think you were right in your assessment of the situation, as regards to the Donkey outthinking us, but I will tell you this. He will be in a rage when he finds out that we have got away and trounced his men to boot. He will concoct a story saying how we were all eliminated, so if you can give the lie to his story he will be discredited further."

Things were getting interesting!

Note from Catherine Whistler. These chapters are not in any way directly related to Space exploration but they concern the leading spacemen and are so important historically that I felt I had to include chapters on the world stage. I hope you all approve.

CHAPTER 27

THE RESISTANCE SUFFERS SOME REVERSES

In the USA the resistance was widely supported and perhaps this led to some overconfidence. The resistances in Europe and America were known to each other but there was at that time no cohesive connection between them. The American resistance there was using the name of Captain Johnson, but he had no executive power. There was a pitched tank battle and the resistance lost. Their fighters were outnumbered yet brave but their lines of supply were not secure enough and they ran out of fuel and ammunition.

Captain Johnson hailed from Boston Massachusetts, and was American through and through. He was both angry and despairing and let it be known that he would accept no more responsibility for that section if they behaved simply as loose cannons. Privately he knew that Americans had a world wide reputation for being gung ho, and that this reputation was deserved. The near collapse of the resistance was a trigger for a revised look at the leadership.

Captain Johnson knew he had the reputation and would be accepted without question, and he further knew that he could leave the British end to those with family ties there. He handed over control to Eric Whistler and took a passenger berth on a freighter to get stateside. He asked Eric Whistler to proceed with all caution until he touched base again. He had no idea if the defeat was a major setback or not but he took no comfort from the news that slowly filtered out.

Life on continental Europe was not good. Many neo Nazis appeared out of no where and helped the Donkey keep a tight grip on things.

The French once again had a fantastic resistance movement and harried the Donkey's men at every opportunity. There was a similar movement in Germany. Although the bulk of the neo Nazis came from there, democracy had given the Germans too many good years to simply die overnight. They went about the business of harrying the Donkey's forces in a logical and well disciplined way. In Britain some very clever men were now part of the resistance movement and Fordy was given the job of overseeing membership.

To his credit he didn't think he had the brains but after a few weeks it was evident that he was making a decent fist of the job.

Nothing was heard of Captain Johnson for almost a month, but the news when it came had a few surprises in it. It is summarised below. It turned out that the American resistance had come under enormous pressure from the wealthy, and had gone head to head with the Donkey's men. This was doomed to failure as the Donkey controlled vast swathes of the American armed forces and the attendant logistics corps as well.

Captain Johnson was incandescent with rage. He wanted to confiscate the wealth from the self serving fools behind the plan, but he was unable to find a good enough reason. He needn't have fretted on this point. The Donkey was so enraged that any organisation would have the sheer front to mount such an operation, that he quickly moved to sequestrate the funds. This move meant a new start in America. Those with that sort of wealth had had it for two or three hundred years, and at a stroke many were reduced to a lowly position overnight.

Captain Johnson ruminated that they would not find it easy to resuscitate their sources of wealth even when the revolution that was coming was confined to the history books.

He smiled inwardly "They will have to work!" Quite a few of the top rich families had money stashed away in Switzerland, but Kingdom Johnson knew there were easy ways to ensure that the rank power of the so called elite could be broken, he decided that he would leave the resistance to carry on with its role of harassing the donkeys men, and leave the Donkey's men to strip the wealth from those who had carelessly thrown away the best chance of overthrowing the Donkey that would come for a while.

He called a meeting of his top guard as they were known.

"Gentlemen, as you know the previous leadership cracked under pressure from within the powerful elite of the USA.

I gather that the sources of wealth that were used to fund this pathetic attempt to kick out the Donkey are being sequestrated at the moment. I concede that the attempt did give the Donkey something to think about, but we lost a lot of our finest lifeblood. When a revolution is attempted again it must be a co-ordinated effort world wide. We in America will probably be expected to give a lead, but not in such an introvert way. I arrived back on this planet having just left a mixed crew on another planet outside the Solar system, so I have an itch there that must eventually be scratched. In the meanwhile I pass to you a paper. In that document you will see I have nominated my replacement and have given a hierarchy that this branch of the resistance *MUST* follow. We must remain iron hard. Normal laws will be restored as soon as possible but in the meantime I, we, are effectively the law. This is a dangerous precedent, but I give you my word that I will step down as soon as the emergency is over. As you see I have added a sworn statement to that effect on the third sheet of your document.

I have thought long and hard about this, and about the political set up that we want when all the shouting is done. I expect many of you will wish to return to normal life, but you may find that inescapable duty binds you to our organisation for some while.

In my view, once the Donkey is defeated, then the old guard will come out of the woodwork and wish or even expect to reclaim their over-privileged positions. No doubt some, the talented few, will succeed, but not without good legal fighting and some very hard work. The moment that the revolution is over, we must lay out our position openly for all to see. This will not be easy. The structure of personnel that I have detailed here has skills from every background. We must engage the best legal minds from England Scotland and the USA. These men will be charged with the duty of providing a sound legal basis that protects both rich AND poor, and the system's adoption will be the key to the dissolution of the resistance prior to reverting to civilian control. It may do us good to remind would be politicians that the Donkey has done us proud and emptied all of our jails, leaving many spaces for us to fill! Now many of the men that he slaughtered will not be missed but there were those who were just in the wrong place at the wrong time. We cannot cure the dissatisfaction and hatred that this will have caused. I am relying on you men to move in an ordered way under my remote direction but I cede to you the powers of a field commander. Have no mercy on Donkey men though I admit that over in England we turned the Donkey's number two, and he has shown considerable skill and fortitude in the battle field already. It would be good if you could find others, but be careful otherwise you will allow the Donkey to infiltrate our organisation! Now then any questions?"

One man raised his eyebrows and took the chair. "Against all my expectations I am now installed as the new leader in the USA. Should any of you break the code of conduct laid out in this document he will be dealt with summarily. Bring me a bible!" he sat down

"Now then swear on oath now that you will uphold the ideals laid down herein." Each man, including himself swore on oath and added his name to the list which was already headed with "Kingdom Johnson"

Within an hour the freighter that was to carry Captain Johnson back to Europe began its run, which would take it via the Suez Canal. The ship never made it. It was over run by piratical men off the coast of Somalia. There had been a resurgence of piracy recently. Captain Johnson couldn't tell if this was an unexpected ploy by the resistance or an actual act of piracy. He was dragged overboard and thrown heavily into the bottom of a small swift heavily armed boat, the boat sped off and its Captain chortled in broken English "we should get a pretty penny for this one! He had no idea of the identity of his prisoner.

A fortnight later a swarthy looking guy turned up in Mogadishu to pay a ransom, but refused to pay a penny until he had seen his target alive and well. Once this was done he roughly handled Captain Johnson who was biding his time and waiting for an opportunity to make his escape. The opportunity never came. He was bound hand and foot and only then when the Captain was shoved roughly into a jeep did money change hands. Captain Johnson knew that he had been handed over to the Donkey's men as soon as money changed hands, and for the first time he began to fear for his life. He heard his captor on a mobile phone saying loudly that he had picked up the goods, and now awaited instructions as to where to make delivery. Half an hour later he heard talk that said he was to be delivered to some address in Egypt in Cairo, but he couldn't quite hear the full details. This would mean a massive overland journey and the jeep was stocked with enough fuel to last for several thousand miles. His captor gave him minimal amounts of water and food but he was going to survive. His inner being was certain of that. On the third day as they bumped along the road, an ancient pre world war two motorcycle passed the jeep going at quite a speed, and it just shot off into the distance and kept going. It was the only thing they saw that relieved the boredom. Every two hours the mobile phone was used to report in. "Package proceeding with all possible speed" said his captor. Another day was coming to a close when a few ramshackle buildings appeared on the road about two miles distant. "You will have a bed to sleep in tonight said the driver; it is my cousin's place!"

This was the only conversation that the driver engaged in. At sunrise the jeep started on the final leg of the overland run it had gone about eight miles when the engine faltered and died. The fuel gauge read zero. The driver refilled from his supplies and went another 15 miles, then spluttered and died again. The fuel tank was again empty. The driver refilled again but after about another twenty miles it was out again. This time the driver took a look at the tank and realised that there was a patch on the fuel tank stuck on with something like chewing gum, and it had simply come half off. The driver phoned in again and kept a level voice as he said "package proceeding with all possible speed." Captain Johnson asked his captor to cut his bonds.

"After all I don't know where I am, this road hasn't been used in years so where am I going to go?"

The driver agreed, and cut his bonds. It took some stiff movements and about twenty minutes before the circulation was properly restored. "How much are they paying you to deliver me?" asked Kingdom quietly. "It is not for the money!" claimed the driver.

"Well I hope the Donkey paid you well, because he wants to be rid of me and he has decided to sacrifice you as well!"

The driver blinked as he added up some basic facts. They were effectively doomed. The nearest humanity was his cousin and in the heat that was an almost impossible trek.

Captain Johnson had looked underneath at the fuel tank and the hacksaw marks were plainly visible. He said "well that patch in the tank isn't a patch. Someone has cut a hole in it by hand. They have used the piece cut out and stuck it back in with chewing gum. That was fuel proof for a while but the combination of petrol and heat and it simply melted and began to leak. The leak got bigger and bigger and now we might have enough fuel to get back to civilisation if only we could repair the tank!"

The driver noticed how Captain Johnson said 'we' and warmed to him in spite of himself. During the cold desert night Captain Johnson slept under the jeep while the driver slept inside. Kingdom was awakened by a finger across his lips to warn of silence and he was instantly alert. The man whoever he was beckoned silently, and two men moved silently away from the jeep and had gone about two miles when his companion said in a thick Australian accent, "well I bloody well thought I would get a better welcome than this from me brother in law!"

"Rod!" exclaimed Kingdom. "What on earth are you doing here?"

"Rescuing you, you bloody useless yank!"

"Well get me the hell out of here then" said Kingdom as he slipped easily into the vernacular.

The motor bike was well muffled now and only made a slight chuffing sound as it went along. "I've been shadowing you ever since you left Mogadishu!" said Rod but I couldn't make a move because you were always tied up!"

"Drive me back to the jeep!" commanded Kingdom. Rod who was Jane's elder brother took the bike as close as he dared and free wheeled for another fifty yards or so, and gave Kingdom a pistol. "You just might need this mate!"

Kingdom Johnson wrenched open the jeep door and woke his captor roughly, pointing the pistol directly at the man's head. He motioned for the driver to get out. The driver though of a swarthy complexion had gone a sort of candle fat grey, accentuated by the moon light.

Captain Johnson said "I am going to give you instructions on how to get back to civilisation and so you shouldn't die. First remove all of your clothing! Right now listen. Use a piece of your shirt to wrap round the patch on the tank and jam it back in the hole. Use plasters from your first aid kit to help tape the patch to the tank and don't worry about slight leaks. If you do that you should make it back and even if you don't the rest should be walkable at night. Now for the moment, start running and don't stop until you can't see the jeep, when you return, I will be gone. Good luck in trying to get back, - off you go!"

The man obeyed and Captain Johnson retrieved the driver's mobile phone from the cab of the jeep he beckoned Rod who threw away the performance sapping muffling around the exhaust outlet and sped up to the jeep. Fortunately the bike had a luggage rack on the back mudguard and so Captain Johnson helped himself to a can of extra fuel from the back of the jeep. At about 60 miles to a gallon that will give us about 1200 miles he said. Rod sniffed in the tank and frowned but said "smells ok."

During the day Captain Johnson used the last number redial function and got a response. "The package is proceeding with all possible speed" doing his best to mimic the jeep driver.

Rod said "you know it took me two days to hack saw that hole out. The metal was thin but the hacksaw was blunt and I had to keep the noise down! The hand drill I had wasn't much better either! With him sleeping inside, I had to wait for him to stir so when the suspension creaked I used the drill to make the four corner holes, after that I spent all night hacking when you were in the ramshackle shed place."

Three days later the mobile phone battery was flat but Captain Johnson was already in northern Europe. He made it back to one of the safe houses, and asked if Jane could be brought to him. Within two hours Jane walked in and saw her brother Rod. She was delighted to see him as she had had very little contact with home since becoming Mrs. Johnson. She was a little disappointed though, but Rod said in his typical dry Australian way. "Don't you go worrying about yer man, I pulled his arse out of the fire some days ago!" just as a door opened and in walked a refreshed smiling Kingdom Johnson.

"I doubt I will ever find your brother a more welcome sight, but tell me how did you know I had been taken?"

Judder had just stepped in to welcome him back and offered, "Fordy still has a few contacts and he let us know that the Donkey was about to pull off a so called 'strategic masterpiece'. The American branch had just informed us of your departure and we let them have the snippet of information. We were deducing that an attempt on your life might be made. A loose mouthed shipping clerk was to blame for blowing your cover, and he has been moved to another job. It was pure conjecture but with you the only senior man on the move and the most vulnerable we put two and two together. Rod was the closest operative but we couldn't get him into Mogadishu in time. The rest you know. Oh by the way that driver you left in the desert did make it back but on foot. His cousin and he returned to the jeep on camelback and then they tried out your suggestion, they got the jeep home on the fuel you left. The man would be of no use to us but at least he thinks you are a better man that the Donkey."

The Donkey's men are every where but we can still move with caution. In the back room of this house we have resistance guys who will help you make a TV appearance; you can decide what you want to say yourself!"

Ten minutes later Captain Johnson stood before a camera, looking very relaxed. He looked into the camera, whilst holding a newspaper and waited for the nod from its operator. He got the nod.

"As you know, I am public enemy number one. Reports of my capture or demise have as usual been exaggerated. He smiled. "That's a wrap!" intoned the technician, as he zoomed in on the date of the newspaper.

CHAPTER 28

THE PENDULUM STARTS SWINGING THE OTHER WAY

The following day the Donkey made another 'personal appearance.'

Putting on his most sincere face he extolled the virtue of the most senior Space Captain and then said "it is with the utmost regret, that I have to report on the death of this hero. He perished in the desert after somehow escaping the re-entry burn up that we all believed he had suffered. This was cruel luck after such a miraculous escape. His image suddenly faded and was replaced by Captain Johnson's short video. Game, set and match to the resistance.

The Donkey was of course under great stress now as it was common knowledge that his erstwhile number two was a member of the resistance and in spite of his best efforts the Donkey was failing to make inroads into the resistance network. He cursed himself for having tried to sacrifice Fordy. He knew it was by his own actions that he had made Fordy doubt him. The resistance had been fragmented into small cells so that if the integrity of one cell was breached the damage stopped there.

The Donkey knew this and knew his days were numbered. He decided on one last big offensive, and he decided that he would inflict his wrath on America. His spy network had been more successful in the USA than anywhere else and a number of cells had been infiltrated. He gave the order to liquidate as many resistance cells as possible.

Unfortunately for him one of his men had successfully been turned and the resistance there had time to take evasive action, and they all went to ground.

Some hours later he was ready in his secure TV transmission studio and he awaited the news from the USA. He was fed false news as his own troops were scared to admit that they had only captured about eight men. In truth they took almost eight hundred men but these were tenants of remote farms and the like. The figure of eight hundred and eight was given to him. He sat in front of the cameras and composed his statement.

"Today we have captured eight hundred and eight resistance fighters. These men and their entire families are to be wiped out. I will not tolerate insurrection. Some months ago there was a poorly organised uprising in the southern states of America. I made plans to ensure that this would never happen again. Those plans are now in an advanced state, and will be implemented during this coming week. The cost of this to my exchequer is enormous and there will be a small increase on general sales tax to fund it! Never again will--- there was a break in transmission and when transmission began again after about half a second, Captain Johnson stood alongside another man.

"I dare say you all know that I am Captain Johnson, and this" he gestured "is Captain Henrik Svensson. We hate to interrupt the latest communiqué from your beloved leader to tell you that he actually did capture some of our men today, eight in all. They were recaptured by the resistance after two hours and are at home with their loved ones as we speak. What a mess! The eight hundred or so who are incarcerated in our near empty jails will be released within a couple of days. The actions of the men who deprived them of their freedom has been noted and the men will be despatched within the next few hours. Remember "Drop the dead Donkey!"

Henrik Svensson then spoke "Remember your cousin the Mule? Well he thought he was clever, and he probably was cleverer than you, Donkey, but he is dead because I shot him to save another greater man. I am coming for you, you will get no sleep. Your body guards are no longer loyal. They fear for their own skins not yours, pleasant dreams."

The normal transmission resumed and caught the Donkey with his mouth agape and he looked not terrified but vacant.

He tried to say a few words but all he managed was a few slurred sounds. He had had a stroke. He died half an hour later. The resistance spread the word of his demise and there were suddenly mass desertions from his security forces.

The resistance was unprepared for the political vacuum that this event created but moved swiftly. All resistance personnel had AK47 or M16 automatics. They were on the street and shot many people as looters struck all over the world. The professional soldiers of the places affected were sworn in as temporary members of the resistance and managed to restore some semblance of order. There was a fair bit of personal revenge taking but the resistance stopped that by the use of kangaroo courts. People were accused, brought before these courts and those found incontrovertibly to be Donkey's men were executed.

It was now safe to come out of the woodwork and many politicals all over the world were soon rabble rousing. The return of freedom was not quite so well established yet and the kangaroo courts dealt quickly with them, and many went straight to prison without a real trial. There would be time for real trials later.

The TV networks were allowed to operate freely once again but the resistance made it plain that they would only permit responsible factual journalism. One or two published stories were simply made up without any basis in fact and the originators joined the slowly growing prison population. The message was getting across.

A number of learned scholars from the legal professions across the world were charged with restructuring the law generally as Kingdom Johnson had wished and they spent many months arguing over small points of law.

Captain Johnson acted on a combined suggestion from the Prof and Judder that earth should take a leaf from the law system operating on mars. This proved a stroke of genius and gave what every body wanted. A system that was simpler to understand and now had a good operating precedent. The learned law scholars approached the resistance requesting remuneration payment.

Fordy of all people had been draughted in as a general paymaster, and he asked them what they expected as the solution to earth's system had come from mars on a suggestion emanating from outside the legal profession, and certainly not from them. To his surprise they accepted that they had not had the expected influence but had had to put in a huge amount of work to translate the Martian system to suit earth's requirements.

Fordy agreed a sum, far less then the legal chaps wanted but far more then some of them dared to hope that they may get.

Fordy gave them another onerous task and suggested that they approach the French and German resistance to see if their legal systems could somehow accommodate the accord that was slowly solidifying in all of the world wide systems that had been based on English law.

The resistance moved quickly to re-establish the banking system, with dire warnings given to that industry. Lloyds of London was held up as a shining example. The money that backed Lloyds up came from 'Names'. These folk stood to make huge amounts of money but could be bankrupted if Lloyds took on bad risks.

All of the world's banks adopted a similar strategy so that no one dropping the banks in the mire by careless activity could then retire on a large protected pension, any pension would depend on the bank's health and this included those who were already retired. No pensions would be funded by companies, but would be funded by persons paying their own sums into their own fund.

This ensured that money in these funds was personal money and was then safe and could not be claimed by a dissatisfied or greedy government, or a crooked entrepreneur. The funds could be traditional pension funds or they could be long term investments where the owner would not have access to withdrawals until he retired. Companies no longer being contributors were no longer able to access pension funds and some of the more gross examples of powerful executives plundering retirement funds were eliminated. That attitude spread through the various civil service organisations and politics as it was accepted that you can not and never should have rewarded failure. The police forces of the world once again became guardians of the peace and were upholders of the law. The courts alone were the law enforcement agencies. The death penalty was found to be used less and less frequently but it would have to stay. It had its opponents who thought it wrong that anyone should be able to give a death sentence out. Its proponents argued that this was correct. They cited the laws of prohibition as an example of a law that sounded good on paper, but was a disaster in practice. It didn't stop the production of alcohol, but put it into the hands of the mob, surely not the original intention. They claimed that in the years when the death penalty had not been operated by the courts the death penalty had been carried out by desperadoes in the streets to further their own ends and it was an abdication of responsibility to rid the state of this option.

A referendum was carried out and the results shocked some of the liberal elite. The death penalty was welcomed by the general public on a 65 35 majority. At the same time corporal punishment was assessed and the public were 55 45 in favour of that, particularly for cowardly attacks on the infirm.

Children were still considered minors and were not legally responsible for the actions; however the parents or guardians were fully responsible, and would go to prison if needs be.

The right of parents to chastise their children were restored and approved though any case of suspected child beating brutality was investigated and the guilty were sent down.

Slowly the law abiding behaviour returned and the more extreme penalties were used decreasingly. They remained on the state statute books however as no–one wanted a return to the crumbling moral decay allowed by the previous so called democratic system.

Many of the points laid out by the worldwide resistance were catered for on a voluntary basis. The world had learnt its lesson, for a while at least.

Helen Johnson extricated the Space administration's funds from Switzerland and went on TV to ask for all former employees to come forward to claim what they were owed. Helen as we all know is no fool but it stretched her intelligence and her patience to the limit whilst grappling with the details of this. The world began to return to something like normal.

China and India never fell to the Donkey but their economies had all but gone bust as they say. With trade links being re-established, disasters were suppressed if not entirely avoided.

At about this point the spacemen resumed their roles in Space administration and exploration.

The Whistler said he could see no space role for himself other than observer but Eric Whistler was ordered to Titan to pick up Peter Ford from the jail there and Captain Johnson would go to rescue the small colony on planet Stellar Two. It took eight months to re organise the

Space control so that a mission could be mounted and it was agreed that the heroes of the resistance would have another party across in England at the Prof's place. "I wonder how his runner beans are doing" thought Captain Johnson, and he now looked forward eagerly to talking over the experiences with his old friend the Prof.

Note from Catherine Whistler. The historians will probably want to flay me alive because I have had to gloss over the enormous difficulties and the titanic struggles to return earth to normal activity, but this story was supposed to be about Space adventure and now it looks as if this tale can continue.

CHAPTER 29

BACK AT THE PROF'S PLACE AND JUST A LITTLE MORE

The Prof was delighted to receive has old friends and their children though a special day out for the children had been organised. This was three days really as they were all going to Euro Disney along with pupils from a local school. The kids really thought this was ace.

With the entire adult group assembled at the Prof's place the Prof had cooked one of his legendary lunches but he had hired a catering company to serve it all up. The Prof took the head of the table with Nadine and Brian Judd nearest him then Eric and Catherine Whistler then Henrik and Helen Svensson and finally Kingdom and Jane Johnson. The Whistler occupied the seat at the far end of the table.

The women looked at each other then chorused "what a swell party this is!" in unison, almost as if they had rehearsed it. For the first evening the conversation was light and did not touch on the serious matters that were the real reason for the party.

Martian elixir flowed as wine should flow and the Prof admitted finding a greater and greater liking for it. The meal of course was topped with the legendary runner beans though these were resuscitated from the Prof's freezer; it was that time of year. The Prof and the Judds were of course still learning about each other but Judder looked slightly uncomfortable as he suddenly got a call on his mobile.

As the meal was fairly well finished Judder stood and spoke "Erm Prof, er Dad," he stuttered "I've got a confession to make. I knew you were hiring staff for the dinner and I've taken a liberty I'm afraid!"

The Prof was in a jovial mood and said "Well speak up then, surely it can't be that bad!"

Nadine, who had only found out about Judder's little liberty earlier in the morning, added "you should have asked me first, but the die is set, spit it out Brian."

Brian Judd turned slightly and beckoned. "Prof I would like to introduce you to my mom!" he said anxiously. The lady who had served the first course looked across at the Prof.

The Prof shot to his feet and immediately offered his chair to the lady who came diffidently across the room, then went to find himself another and dragged that up to the table.

"I feel so awkward about this Prof" she spoke softly "as I know I am not his real mom."

The Prof gallantly said "you may not be his mother but you are most certainly his mom!"

She looked at the Prof and relaxed and said "Brian told me I would like you and he was right." Neither the Prof nor Elizabeth noticed as the others left the dining room, and were deeply engrossed in their own conversation.

"I think we have a lifetime of little things to discuss, and with any luck that is also what it should take" smiled the Prof as he warmed to this gentle lady. He reached for his wallet and fetched out a rather battered photograph of his former wife and after glancing at it, Elizabeth rummaged inside her bag and produced an equally battered photograph of herself. "We could have been friends" she said "and really we do look rather alike." Suddenly a look of dawning spread across her features. "Yes we really *did* look *alike*. *That is why after the quake a hotel porter thrust Brian into my arms and stopped me from protesting that he wasn't mine saying he was glad that he was certain that Brian was mine because he had seen me with him the day before.* He knew I was confused and put my attitude down to that. I thought that his parents had been unlucky and been killed so we stayed on locally in a caravan that escaped the worst of the devastation and I hoped that his mom and dad would reclaim him. Nothing happened and I finally decided that I and my husband couldn't give him up to orphanhood and we brought him up.

The Prof had been alone for many years now and he went straight to the point with a directness that floored her. "Elizabeth, I need a girlfriend, will you do me the honour!"

She then surprised herself and said simply "Yes!"

They joined the others out in the Prof's conservatory and walked out arm in arm.

"I say steady on mom!" joked Judder, "I never knew my dad was such a fast worker!"

Nadine came across and spoke quietly to Elizabeth. "Mom, I'm so sorry that Brian went about this in such a clumsy way, I think I would have had a little more finesse if only he had kept me posted!"

"Nadine, I knew you were the man for Brian as soon as you came to our house that day and I concede that you are far more subtle in your approach than Brian will ever be, but in this case I am chuffed that the evening has rolled along as it has, after all I didn't come here expecting to get a boyfriend, but it seems I've got one now! I suppose getting me to join the team of caterers was Brian's idea of subtlety."

Nadine grinned and said "well I'm sure you will have plenty in common and a more charming man you will never find! He almost charmed me off my feet when I first met him and I found the old sod so likeable it was almost painful. He may have a few miles on his clock but there is plenty of life in him yet! When Brian and I found ourselves at this house and it became evident that Brian had achieved recognition, we both felt regret that you weren't here to see that but now you should have a front row seat for anything else that he does!"

"Well, it is good to have a family and the Prof hasn't had one and yet, I don't know, something inside tells me that we haven't got entirely to the bottom of this yet!" with that Elizabeth sought out James Whistler and thanked him profusely for having a good enough memory to recall the earth quake issue because without that, the link between the Prof, Brian and Elizabeth would never have come to light.

Elizabeth had come from a broken family and had been fortunate enough to be adopted. The laws on adoption were administered in a most unfriendly way in those days and she never knew who her real parents were. Her adoptive parents both dead now, had brought her up in ideal conditions and she had grown into a well rounded character, and yet deep down inside her she did feel the need to know a little more of her roots. When her own husband died she had been bereft, and all such ideas had been banished from her waking thoughts. However, time is a good healer, and once again her mind turned to this issue.

That evening the Prof gave her a tour of his garden and told her of his passion for runner beans and roses and then gave her a guided tour of his large house.

She commented "this is a beautiful house but it must be lonely when there is only you here!"

The Prof had a small lump in his throat as he agreed then said "this here is my room" as he opened the door. "I will prepare the end bedroom for you Elizabeth and I suppose I had better get on with that or you will have nowhere to sleep!"

Elizabeth stood stock still and almost against her will said "do I need a separate room then?"

The lump in the Prof's throat subsided but was replaced by another lump from an entirely different emotion. He closed the door.

....

The following morning they rose for breakfast quite early and had eaten theirs before anyone else came down.

They had found a passion for each other that neither knew was in themselves until that night and it showed.

Nadine came down next and her face split with an enormous grin as she saw them sitting close together. "Perhaps Brian's approach really did a better job than mine would have" she thought.

The Prof spoke earnestly and openly to Elizabeth. "When this party is over and everyone goes, I don't want you to go Elizabeth. I want you to stay!"

"I will be delighted to do that Bill, but I must take care of my house down in Gloucestershire, I can't just buzz off!"

Bill Wild AKA the Prof smiled and said "well the next best thing then is if I go with you to Gloucestershire and help you sort things out!"

The rest of the day was taken up with discussions on the forthcoming Space venture and Elizabeth listened avidly. She noticed the Prof earnestly talking to James Whistler and presumed this was more of the same. The third and final day belonged to the Space captains. Just for once Henrik was to fly as second in command to Captain Johnson and Eric Whistler was to revisit Titan. James Whistler was absent for most of the day. He turned up at the end of the day and gave an envelope to the Prof saying "well I hope you are ok with this because I have uncovered something that could really upset you!"

The Prof cast a quick glance round the room and made his exit unnoticed. Up in his room he opened the envelope and read it carefully, twice. "Come in" he said to the knock that came on his door. "Here you are!" exclaimed Elizabeth, "I thought you had run out on me!"

"Never!" said the Prof, "please, you had better read this!"

Elizabeth read it three times and she drew a deep breath. "YOU really are a fast worker!" She looked at him and put him at his ease. She nodded her head in wonderment. "Did James Whistler really dig this up in just a few hours?"

"He did, and thinking back now, if that earth quake had only come a couple of days later we may have met each other then. When Mary died it was before the great DNA data base was created so we will have no solid way to prove this but it really does look as though Mary was your sister. The likeness was so apparent to that waiter that he didn't realise that there were two people. The rest we already know. You do know, don't you that after a respectful time I am going to ask you something?"

"My answer will be yes, so don't leave it too long!" said Elizabeth, but I have to break the news to Brian. By the way why is everybody calling him 'Judder'?"

The Prof explained how a spaceship shakes just as it makes the jump and how Brian had tried to calm a few nerves by saying "never mind the judder, it always happens with a successful jump". Now with a name like Judd, his nickname was self creating and it stuck. "Hardly anyone calls me by my name, I am the Prof."

"Well it will always be Bill and Brian to me" said Elizabeth sticking out her still pretty chin.

They returned to the lower level and Elizabeth sought out Brian and Nadine, the Prof however sought out Catherine Whistler. When the group was assembled Elizabeth gave them all the latest news. Brian was almost agape. "You really aren't making this up are you?" he asked.

Catherine Whistler asked if she could see the old photographs and then went quiet.

"What's the matter Catherine?" asked Elizabeth.

Catherine swallowed twice before answering. "Surely you can see that they were twins? Look at the smile. The one front tooth is very slightly bigger than the other but they are mirror images and I'm sure that only happens with twins!"

Elizabeth had blanched. She muttered how she had gone through a period in her late forties when she had felt at death's door then spoke aloud as she turned to face the Prof. "That must have been when your beloved Mary died. I couldn't explain how low I felt and it went on for some months but finally I just recovered."

The Prof hit his mobile and spoke calmly "James we thought it may narrow the search somewhat if you look for orphaned twins who were split up shortly after their birth."

He looked around the little group and said "I must be losing it. Why on earth didn't I realise that myself!" Captain Johnson had heard most of what was said and chimed in "I wouldn't worry about that too much Prof, I couldn't even recognise my own daughter when she stood in front of me. A lady member of the undercrew had no problem in realising Helen had my blood in her veins and said so. I felt such a pillock for not realising something so obvious that it upset my self belief for days!"

Elizabeth thought quietly to herself that the hotel waiter had been so nearly correct and how she had thought at the time that her desire to bring up the orphaned child was simple mothering instinct but now she thought it may just have run a little deeper than that. She had had an aching void in her soul that she had never been able to come to terms with, but perhaps now the jigsaw was finally coming together. She looked across at the Prof and realised that they had been fated to meet sooner or later, and she knew she would soon be Mrs. Wild. She looked forward to it but she didn't want a big wedding. Her life had suddenly gone from almost empty to overflowing and she felt what she supposed was satisfaction. It was a new feeling.

The Prof then said gently "Elizabeth you may just be wondering why I brought Catherine Whistler into our little group. It started with her grandfather who wrote the story of early Space travel, well when he retired Catherine took over the job so I dare say we will figure somewhere in her account. She has to archive all of the interminable reports from Space and she tries to extract the story of adventure from it all. Recently the job has become so big that she has used Jane Johnson to help her out. Now her story essentially concerns Space travel but those in this room have become so central to the story that there will be a few chapters on the Donkey I am sure, and I dare say our little story will appear in there somewhere."

Elizabeth was quite thrilled and went over to find Catherine and talk some more to her.

Elizabeth was pleased to find that each of the women attached to the Space exploration men, were characters in their own right, not the dreadfully shallow types depicted as being 'normal' on so many "reality" TV shows. She knew she was now one of a well rounded crowd, and she borrowed a copy of Catherine's first book to read it.

After a couple of hours she had been through most of it then suddenly shrieked with laughter and said "cheeky cow!"

"Who is?" enquired Catherine Whistler.

"You are. Fancy asking the King of England to endorse the story, did he do it?"

"Read on and you will find he really did" said Catherine, "in fact without that I would have had a devil's game to get a publisher to take it on."

"Elizabeth grinned and said "well they do say fortune favours the bold!" and she burst once again in to delighted laughter.

Catherine replied, "Don't forget you will be in the second book!" and the two women laughed together. The first book had only sold moderately until the last interview that Captain Johnson had given, whilst a member of the earth interim government. This was beamed and syndicated almost worldwide and in the interview he mentioned that anybody who wanted to know just the general details of the recent upheavals would do well to read the book by Catherine Whistler as soon as it was published, but really to get a flavour of the characters of the Space service who were so deeply involved, they could do no better than to read Catherine's first book which was already in all good book shops. He also mentioned that the story had been endorsed by the English King, King Charles. Enquiries went through the roof and many advance orders were taken bringing in so much wealth that Catherine was better off than her husband.

CHAPTER 30

ONE TOUGH LADY

Catherine was well aware that many literary critics whose acid tongues far outweighed their literary originality, would want to tear her down by over-dissecting her work so she composed a preface disclaiming any literary skill. In spite of many barbed comments from the critics, or possibly helped by these comments she received the sort of acclaim that any writer cannot do without. Her book soon sold well. She decided she would publish a second book once she had distilled what she could from the imminent story that was about to unfold.

She agreed to do just one TV interview and the man conducting the interview was known for his abrasive style. He was all sweetness and light until the cameras started to roll, and then he tore into her and made slanderous attacks on her character for no apparent reason. Catherine, indignant at the unprovoked attack, was on fire inside but she kept outward calm and said "well why don't you go and try to do better, then when your book sells really well you will be able to interview your self and destroy your own character then we could all be rid of you!"

There was a silence broken only by the stifled laughter of the studio crew. He said nothing.

Catherine then said, "don't forget this is the post Donkey era, and you have no right to expect to make such scurrilous comments and get clean away with it. In fact you could end up in jail. Now there's a thought!"

She thought for a moment more and then added "I'll tell you what, I'll interview *you* right now and you can explain to the viewers why you wanted to do a hatchet job on me!"

There was a silence. He tried to speak but the words died in his throat.

Catherine was a humorous woman but she was also intelligent and deductive, and suddenly a little light burned brightly. "Deny that you are related to the Donkey!"

He had gone tallow fat yellow and again he tried to speak but no intelligible words came out.

"Oh just get out of my sight!" said Catherine. The cameras moved to one side and focussed purely on Catherine Whistler as the now silently blubbering interviewer was removed and replaced by his understudy.

The cameras finally turned onto the understudy. He was grinning widely. "That is the best TV interview I have ever seen" he said smiling at Catherine. "Do you know if he is in fact related to the Donkey?" he added.

"No of course not, but I knew he must have absolutely hated the ground I stand on and it occurred to me that such a relationship may explain his outrageous attitude towards me."

"Well I have read your book, it is a good read and I must say that your grandfather could take much of the credit for the story!"

Catherine's eyes softened and she said, "He must have the 100% credit for the early part of it and for setting the ground rules in how the book was composed. I only finished it off just after he died, and before you ask, yes I did ask King Charles if he would endorse the story." The interview then went according to the normal way of things as the understudy made a superb job of interviewing her, and she warmed to this man's polite charm.

Just at the end he openly invited her to comment further on the initial part of the interview and she was candid.

"I had no idea of the fate that he had decided I should face, he was so polite back stage, two faced or what? I must congratulate you, young man on turning a very nasty situation round and I trust your employers will recognise your efforts."

He then added "Well I can understand why Eric Whistler chose you as his wife, you are one formidable lady. Will you be pressing charges?"

Catherine Whistler grinned. "What, press charges against a minor? I think that may be against the law! I still can't really believe he said what he said; I mean what on earth got into him?"

There were other issues though that needed settling in a more traditional way. One punch from Eric Whistler and the interviewer was out cold. The punch was done in the toilet block and Eric Whistler merely retired to a toilet cubicle, and waited for the interviewer to stagger back out side and the hubbub to die down then merely went and sat back in his car and awaited Catherine.

When she came back he said "It looks like the Donkey had a narrow escape from you!" he leant across and kissed her. "I have never seen such a crass and overbearing cowardly fool brought down so easily, I am really proud of you!"

She shook with rage and then burst into tears for a few seconds, but she was one tough lady and soon recovered her composure. On the way out the security guard recognised her and saluted before asking for and receiving her autograph. He raised the barrier, they were on their way and that was that. They didn't enquire as to the fate of the erstwhile abrasive interviewer.

CHAPTER 31

HENRIK SPENDS A DAY OR TWO ORBITING VENUS

Henrik was despatched via the latest mark of shuttle to normalise the crews on the big Space ships, which were still orbiting Venus.

He was welcomed by the skeleton crews as a conquering hero, which he modestly denied.

"I played my part, but there were thousands of others involved. Anyway how do you know what has been going on, there was a virtual radio blackout?"

"We took a leaf from Judder's book and used shuttles to go into lunar orbit then used our mobiles, so we are aware that earth has now almost returned to normal!"

"Earth will never be quite the same again. Many of the wealthy have been stripped of their wealth by the Donkey, and the constitution of the civilised world is now such that the only way they are going to become wealthy again is by working. You guys will have a fair bit of back pay to claim but you won't get it immediately. My wife is in charge of that function, and it is only due to her that you or I will have any money due. She read the vibes just before the big upheaval and salted the Space administration's funds away in the Swiss banking system. She was public enemy number one because of her actions. She survived. Do any of you remember Peter Ford?"

"I remember him, he sided with the mule and went to jail on Titan!" came a voice from the back of the room.

"Well he had a twin brother called Donald. Don Ford is known by the nickname of 'Fordy'. He was actually the Donkey's number two. He became disenchanted as he realised that the Donkey was simply a megalomaniac, and he took an appalling risk by openly declaring that he knew how to get rid of him. The resistance boys snaffled him and he hated all of us. He hated the Donkey and he hated the Space administration and he hated the previous so called democratic governments. He had been told by the Donkey that his brother had been ejected into Space and when Captain Johnson let it be known that was not true, Fordy embraced the resistance wholeheartedly. He fought with distinction during the grim days, and he has given a good account of himself in one or two awkward jobs given him since then.

I am up here to start the relief of you lads, though anyone that wants to remain on board can do so. Captain Whistler is going to Titan because Fordy has earned a temporary reprieve for his brother, and I am going as number two with Captain Johnson to relieve the colony left on Stellar two.

Now then has anybody been ill? No? Good! It is planned that the Gravitas will return to earth lunar orbit but the Solar Orbiter and the Space Adventurer, will go on the missions I have described. We will have to spend some time re-crewing the two ships so let's get on with it. Firstly give me a list of all those wishing to stay on board." He was greeted with wide grins but the list when presented had no names on it.

"Just thought I'd ask!"

Henrik settled his command on the Gravitas and gradually organised the re-crewing of the other two ships. This took almost three weeks and involved the transport of some 35000 persons the majority of whom were in the undercrews. The undercrews did not reap the glory of the operational crews but were well respected non the less, as the smooth running of all of the missions so far undertaken was down in large part to their unselfish actions. There were some very skilled personnel in the undercrew and they all knew that they could be pressed into operational duties if ever the need arose.

With both ships now fully crewed and gradually getting their feel for the job back again Henrik Svensson allowed himself a two day break back on earth with his family. After that the missions began in earnest.

CHAPTER 32

ON THE SPACE ADVENTURER.

Eric Whistler returned to the bridge of this ship as if he had never been away. He spoke to the entire crew over the ship communications video.

"Ladies and gentlemen, welcome aboard for our latest venture. This venture will only involve one jump in each direction and the primary purpose of it is to visit Titan to see for ourselves how the colonisation is going. Many of you will know that the work there is largely carried out by earth prisoners. There are no chains used in normal prison life, after all where can they go? The prison system is really a social experiment but like any other it will fail unless sufficient willpower and diligence is used in its upkeep. Normally visits by earth ships were every two or three months, but due to the upheavals on the home planet no one has been there for almost three years, and we have had no communiqués from there either.

I must admit that the harshness of decisions that I have had to take during the period of unrest was against my general philosophy in life but I will take them again if I have to. We are not expecting any trouble, but it will be met with craft guile and stiff resolve if there is any. Eric Whistler out!"

The ship was fired up on rocket power and then used its gravity motor to get back to a black hole between earth and mars. The jump went without a hitch and the ship was soon in orbit round Saturn. Eric Whistler decided he would learn as much as he could before attempting landfall. He noted that the farming tents had now spread over quite an area, and he could just about detect human movement with the ships sensors at maximum amplification. He studied the goings on for two days before hailing.

It took quite a while before a response came. The video screen showed a bearded man who was plainly relieved. "You took your time we had honestly thought that we had been abandoned."

"I am afraid that earth has undergone a savage revolution and an even more savage restructuring, but things are slowly returning to normal. Are you clear to accept a shuttle?"

"We are, but our earth supplied stocks are running out!"

"Ok, we will make a full inventory and replenish where ever required, Whistler out."

The following day a few common supplies like vacuum packed bacon and tins of beer were loaded into the shuttle and our good old friend Heinrich was put in command of the away team.

Down on Titan the away team was made to feel welcome. The prisoners had done a good job but some had been there longer than there nominal sentence and understandably wanted to get back to their families on earth.

Heinrich asked to see Peter Ford, and was introduced to the bearded man seen on the video link. Peter was hungry for news of Don and opened the envelope that he was given impatiently. He read the temporary pardon that he had been offered and said, "I will need to speak to my team here before I agree to any thing." Peter Ford had been a man of some ability and when earth visits had stopped he had been voted as the chairman, much to his surprise. He now regarded the Titanese colony as his team, and was well respected. It seemed that the hopelessness of their position had given quite a number of them a new lease of life.

The social anthropologists down on earth would rave about the success of the colony but for all their high faluting theory it was obvious that it was teamwork that had had brought about success. That night a dinner was served and there was a starter using the bacon just brought down along with another meat dish that Heinrich likened to schweinfleisch, or wild boar. It was of course moonpork from the moonpig.

Peter Ford said "we decided to try that quite early on because it would eke out our dwindling supplies and in fact it has made us almost totally independent from earth. We tried eating the worms and the flying crab things but they are both totally unpalatable. The nuclear station is still working nicely and any spare energy from that is used to keep our tents warm, so at the moment we can harvest not only what we sow but also the minerals and gases that make this place unique.

Eric Whistler sanctioned the landfall of the few who had volunteered for a spell on Titan, and they were made to feel doubly welcome. He let it be known that it was likely that their community would be swelled out by the arrival of disenfranchised politicians in the not too distant future.

This gave considerable mirth to some of the prisoners. The widely grinning faces and shaking of heads as the community really looked forward to 're-educating the cretins of earths failed system' as one man put it.

"There really is nothing like this place. You either help your neighbours or you won't survive. No clever words are much use here. You have to work hard, but the rewards are self evident. I am simply not the man that was sent here all those years ago!" so said Peter Ford.

When Eric Whistler spent two days on the surface he noticed an odd sort of cloakroom and asked what it was for.

Peter Ford said "Ah! Mr. Whistler, you are not the only one who can invent things you know! We have your design for a man powered flight device but one day I thought that it may be better to just provide a glider. We got our heads together and we designed a sort of kite that you can strap on your back. You then run and skip into the air and you can fly about two hundred yards like that. There is a technique involved, and a couple of times now we have held what we call our flying fish contest, a sort of sports day. We have great fun; the winner last time managed a flight of about a quarter of a mile!"

Fast forward now to earth some days later, Peter Ford stepped out from the shuttle as he stepped onto earth again. His legs felt unbelievably weak but he managed to walk across as he spotted Fordy standing on the tarmac.

The two men embraced and appeared to be in extremely good spirits; Peter was effusive in his praise for Don. But surprised him by saying "If I had stayed on Titan for another couple of years I would have elected to stay there!"

Fordy though was quick to reason why. "No politics?" Peter smiled and nodded in the affirmative.

Back on the Space Adventurer, Eric Whistler felt at a loose end, he wanted something to do.

An idea occurred to him relating to the fireball seen in Stellar two system. He wondered whether he could divert the fireball into the Solar system then perhaps guide it to take up an orbit near Triton, or even Ganymede.

He sent a despatch to the Johnson –Svensson mission asking for their opinion. It took many hours to get a reply, but a reply did come.

Captain Johnson urged caution but the Whistler was keen.

"Now there's a turn up for the book "he thought. He realised that they were not against the idea and were leaving the decision up to him.

After some deliberation his course of action was clear, he decided he would catch up with the Stellar two expedition, ask the Whistler to accompany him and then seek out the fireball.

He asked for volunteers for the mission and was pleasantly surprised that over ninety percent jumped at the offer. Others were not against it but there were family reasons that most that elected not to go this time could not escape.

He knew that there was more stretch potential in the undercrew and asked for volunteers to fill the few vacant operational crew vacancies.

Within ten days his mission was under weigh.

The jumps were made without incident and he left progress reports at every comms jump ship on his route.

In terms of galactic travel times he had soon caught up with the main mission, and hailed the Solar Orbiter.

"What kept you?" was the response "close ranks to within visual distance." Was his order, "then come aboard!"

He complied and brought Captain Johnson up to date with the completion of his own mission.

Kingdom Johnson was pleased that the jail on Titan seemed just for once to be successful and he was surprised at just how well the Titans had done. He then brought Eric Whistler up to date with regard to the Stellar two position. Here was an unexplained issue.

Every person on the colonial team had aged by possibly ten years, they had all recorded a stay of about nine years but the earth time passing was only about six years.

"Do you remember when Judder first made contact with Nadine she said he had been away for three and a half years whereas our clocks had only advanced by seven to eight months?," enquired Captain Johnson.

Eric Whistler nodded in the affirmative.

"Well James Whistler is struggling to find any possible scenario where this could have happened. We know it did happen, and our suspicion is that a lifetime on Stellar two may only be about seventy percent of an earth lifetime. Having said that; the colonialists have successfully brought seven children into being. They have also done well survival wise. They now have decent sized farms and the Prof's runner beans are at least as good as they would be back home.

There is life in the oceans on this planet but the flesh, if we can call it thus, is of very low density and is just about invisible to our detectors. We have released some fish from our on board aquaria and these swam off at great speed, we do not know of the success of their survival at present, but one fish was kept in a netted area for a week and seemed perfectly ok so we have high hopes there.

One of the colonialists was a student of botany and he has decided the planet would benefit from trees, so he has planted some pines. Pines were chosen because of their ability to stand extremes of climate. These have spread, not exactly like a rash. But they are doing ok. We have our engineers working on providing some canoes so that ocean exploration can be attempted. On some future mission we plan to introduce pigs to provide another source of meat. If successful we will consider other livestock. Before you ask I used the word 'another' when talking of meat. The colonialists already have one source. One thing we didn't check on when choosing the personnel here was if any of them had pets. One woman had a pet hen. Well a cockerel must have got at her because she laid some eggs and the settlers kept the eggs warm and the fertilised ones hatched. The result was four little chicks survived. They now have a flock numbering about seventy and a regular supply of fresh eggs. Initially they used human food to keep them alive but they found out that the local seaweed was nutritious and the chickens like it. This planet does have the ability to support earth life in most forms. Now one or two settlers have had stinking colds, so the cold virus is already out and about.

We have just donated mushroom spores from our on board farms and time will tell if the planet can support fungi."

"Wow!" said Eric Whistler.

"The Stellar two people are unaware of the time slippage so for the moment we would like to keep it that way!" ordered Captain Johnson.

Eric Whistler lowered his voice. "Erm Kingdom I would like to ask you an enormous favour," he continued, "I was wondering whether it would be a good idea to try to harvest that fireball that nearly saw us off and try and divert it so that we send it to the Solar system and get it to orbit Ganymede.

"Yes you mentioned that in your communiqué. What does the favour involve?"

"I would like to borrow my grandfather for the duration of my self imposed mission!"

Captain Johnson went quiet as he considered this. "I suppose chasing that fireball is connected to this mission in a loose kind of way. He picked up the general communication microphone "bridge here, bridge here, James Whistler to the bridge please!"

Minutes later James Whistler was in the bridge area and smiled broadly as he shook his grandson's hand with some force in his grip.

"James, Eric here has asked if I would second you to the Space Adventurer while he chases the fireball, and I wonder if you would consider it."

"Actually I was thinking that I might just make some inroads into my present problem if I could find a new point of attack. Perhaps this would be what I need. I have felt stale for a few days now, no doubt because I am failing to make any progress."

Eric Whistler said "well Grandad, I could not swear to this but just as the Solar Orbiter made the jump that let the fireball out of its entrapment, I was struggling with the usual lack of manoeuvrability of the Space Adventurer when the manoeuvrability was suddenly almost gone completely. I hit the rocket throttles a fraction of a second before Henrik and I got into the rethe just before he did, but I wonder if this time slippage was something to do with the fireball!"

"Why was this not in your report!" scowled Captain Johnson.

"It has taken me some weeks to extract it from my memory and even that may be part of the phenomenon" replied Eric Whistler.

"Anybody but you and I would have laughed in their face", grinned Captain Johnson, "but I do know how honest you are, and perhaps we should give a line of research such as this the highest priority!"

James Whistler's face had assumed its glacial expressionless appearance and the other two chuckled.

"It looks like he has volunteered then!" said Captain Johnson, "Orbiter to Gravitas, Orbiter to Gravitas," he called.

Henrik Svensson's face appeared on the screen. "Henrik if you would like to get over to here we have things we need to discuss!" intoned Captain Johnson.

Minutes later Henrik walked in and shook Eric Whistler's hand. "Fancy meeting you here!" he quipped.

Captain Johnson outlined the new mission strategy which now involved Eric Whistler and told Henrik of the Whistler's desire to join the Space Adventurer.

Henrik stood stock still as he listened to his update and suddenly a look dawned on his face. "I have had something at the back of my mind ever since we made that out of sequence jump" he said "but it was elusive and I kept thinking about it spasmodically. It was very irritating because I did not know or rather could not recall what was bothering me, but that was it. It was the sudden total absence of manoeuvrability just as the fireball appeared. It was there only for seconds and as shear survival instinct blotted out everything else it has just lain there as a dormant grub, in the back of my mind. Every time it wriggled it upset me but I could not bring it to my cognisant mind. Thanks Eric, I might get a better night's sleep now!"

The Whistler rose from his reverie and commented "if that fireball is positive matter containing a small amount of negative matter we may have a zero time zone contained within an ether time zone. God only knows what that might entail, but we will have to be careful.

I suggest that when the stellar two mission is complete and you would otherwise have returned to earth that you join us in our investigations. It is possible that we may have come upon the real reason that Sonny shines. I have never been entirely happy with even the latest theory as to why that is so. I feel that we are on the verge of finding out why the time within the number two Solar system is not running as we expect. This is an exciting moment!"

Captain Johnson agreed and wrote out his command instructions so that every man in that room knew what his responsibilities were. Copies of the new mission instructions were handed round.

"Eric, it is down to you that this extension of our mission is being undertaken, I must impress upon you to curb the hotter of your pursuit traits, in the name of Space service safety!"

"I accept that in full Captain Johnson, and I beg you to remember I will have the Whistler aboard so seeing as he is my Grandad, I will use my utmost endeavours to protect us all from harms way."

CHAPTER 33

THE STELLAR TWO MISSION TIES UP A FEW LOOSE ENDS

The engineering facility on board the two ships produced some lightweight canoes, and provided fishing nets and fishing rods. They also made a more substantial vessel about one hundred feet long. It had a mast and a sail with an anchor and a decent keel. This was assembled down on the surface and then launched by slip function. The ship stood proudly in a bay riding at her anchor. None of the settlers knew how to sail, but Henrik Svensson himself did and he gave quite a number of lessons, finally knowing that at least six of the settlers had the rudimentary sailing skills.

The settlers had a copy of the Mars manual. This detailed how the mars mission slowly became independent of earth. Possibly another nuclear station could be a way forward, but in the meanwhile the lenses, mirrors and photovoltaic elements were constructed to provide a small source of electricity. The original mission had left a sizeable battery system, and the settlers had also produced a small wind farm to supplement supplies.

Henrik was a free thinking type of man and he asked Captain Johnson if it was possible to leave a geostationary satellite in orbit with mobile phone functions set into it. The on board engineers soon came up with a design but it took another six weeks to complete and test it for functionality. Each settler was given a mobile phone of the new solar powered types and everyone had a list of the numbers. Settlers were delighted as it took them back out of the Stone Age at a stroke. They had given all of the exploration data to Captain Johnson as the second visit got under weigh and apologies for the meagre amount done; explaining that fear for the safety of their comrades had kept them on a short leash. Now with easy mobile phone links this fear was removed to a degree. A single satellite would not give planet wide coverage, but it was a start. Future visits could improve the situation.

Now the planet's food and fuel supplies had been somewhat depleted and these were replenished and increased. The two captains asked for and got many interested folk to volunteer for a stay on Stellar two.

Each volunteer had to go through a stringent vetting procedure as a mistake in choice could spell disaster for the colonists. Again an equal mix of male and female participants were selected, and then given a three week trial period before being finally left to their own devices, for a fortnight. Every one of the volunteers came through this selection procedure with flying colours. The newcomers totalled one hundred souls in all, two of whom were doctors. This was a move in the right direction as far as Stellar two folk were concerned.

The planet's trees were if not flourishing growing ok. The botanist had seen fit to plant a minor amount of other trees and he requested some livestock to fill the void as far as wild creatures were concerned. Squirrels and magpies were left there. Both of these creatures were curious and intelligent and if any creature could survive on its own, these would have as good a chance as any. The last gift bestowed upon the settlers was an Eden shelter storeroom stocked with hand tools, drills, saws, nails, and a myriad of other earthly items and some screws. Also left were a couple of small machine tools and a supply of extruded metals so that with a bit of ingenuity the settlers could manufacture things themselves. As an afterthought three mountain bicycles were left with several sets of spare tyres and inner tubes and puncture outfits, and finally a number of spare mobile phones.

As his last act at this stage, Captain Johnson went down onto the surface to talk to the settlers about the new tail end to this mission.

He candidly spoke of the time element conundrum at the end of the original Stellar two mission, and how he had sent two of his best senior men, namely the Whistlers, off chasing a possible solution.

The settlers were informed of the decreased life expectancy they would suffer unless the conundrum could be solved. He also said that the decreased life expectancy may only be two or three percent, (economic with the truth here) and that may well be countered by the environmental cleanliness that they all enjoyed (pure educated guesswork here). The effect though was to pump adrenaline into the morale of the settlers. The life expectancy issue was not at the front of anyone's mind because they were all still so young, and frankly they all thought that Captain Johnson was exaggerating a little.

Captain Johnson asked if there was anything that was unusual on this planet, and the answer was the absence of a moon. This made the night time very dark, and the women candidly declared that their periods were quite irregular. So the good old moon on earth did have a regulatory effect on women. Not one person expressed any serious worries so Captain Johnson offered them another visit from earth in three earth years. He also left several fuel refills for the shuttle, and a print out of the latest details of Stellar 2 charting.

The settlers gave a resounding cheer as Captain Johnson left and settled back immediately into their new way of life, but now with sufficient wherewithal to explore the planet more fully. So far the settlers had not used any of the mineral resources of the planet. The new arrivals though had the skills to promote issues of that sort and so a naissance was expected.

The two Space ships orbited until they were pointing in the right direction and then started chasing the Space Adventurer.

CHAPTER 34

THE MISSION REACHES FULL STRENGTH

The Gravitas made the first jump followed shortly afterwards by the Solar Orbiter. When they exited the rethe an attempt at hailing the Space Adventurer produced no results. Both captains looked at their on board computors and realised that the fireball was travelling so fast and thus so far that another jump could be made. They made it and ended up ahead of the fireball. This time hailing brought an almost instant response and all three ships registered on each other's radar.

Eric Whistler now deemed the leader of this latest escapade ordered the three ships into close formation and called for a three way head to head to be held on the Space Adventurer.

Aboard the lead ship when all of the captains were there, the three captains also sought opinions from the Whistler and Judder.

Eric let it be known that he had found it almost impossible to get too near to the fireball, and members of his undercrew had complained that they found it difficult to move at their usual speeds. It was like the nightmare when something is chasing you and a force is preventing you from getting away. His ship would not respond to its controls and even with rocket motor assistance things were barely any better. He could get close enough to affect the target with the pull of his gravity motor, but he had reasoned that the only safe way to pull it into a new course was to use a three pronged pull. He believed that if they did this it would pull the fireball which would then pass between them on its new course. He was delighted that the others had decided to join him in this venture because he had been on the point of aborting his mission.

The Whistler however was very excited.

"I have been studying the fireball as and when we got as close to it as we could and in my view there is an extremely interesting reaction going on in it. We have all experienced the eddy current effect of loss of control which we discovered and explained some time ago. In point of fact there is no actual loss of control, it is still there. The ship will do exactly as it should but it responds more slowly. Now when we are close to our target the response is so dreadfully slow that it appears to be not responding at all.

Previously, when we have experienced this it was because we were in a gravity neutral zone close to a black tunnel, and as the ship traversed the massive concentration of gravity lines at the jump point it induced this sluggishness. The peculiar thing in this case is that we are not anywhere near a black tunnel portal. We must however be at a point where the concentration of gravity lines is particularly dense. The dense gravity lines are therefore a part of the physicality of the fireball."

Judder interrupted, "Well if that fireball is composed of matter and antimatter in equal proportion, is it not likely that there would be a sort of oscillation from one to the other and back again as each tries to swallow the other?"

The Whistler grinned "You really are like your dad! That was the next point in my conjecture. There is a continuous exchange between the two worlds and as the matter rushes into the anti matter zone it upsets the balance. The anti matter then gets the upper hand and so it causes a rush in the opposite direction. Now so far is I can tell both actions are going on simultaneously and in a sort of random ball. Not only that, quite unlike a simple resonance, there are multiple frequencies going on. Each paired piece of matter-antimatter undergoes an oscillatory behaviour but the frequencies vary according the proximity of one to the other. At any instant there is an exactly equal amount going in each direction, this governed by the law of existence balance. There are millions of particle collisions that then give off heat, but the beauty of it is that positive particles can collide with negative or positive particles but can only combine with negative particles and the exact balance of one to the other is maintained. The reaction is even more efficient than a nuclear fusion reaction. The outer extremities are composed of heavy atoms such as iron and uranium and are providing a long life source of positive particles. I have to assume at this stage that there is a matching source of negative particles other wise the reaction would not balance and would have been over in the blink of an eye. I don't profess to have found a full explanation at this juncture but I'm still working on it! There must be a savage concentration of gravity lines inside the ball and the incoming lines from the ether are so concentrated near the ball that we lose our mobility! The oscillatory action seems to generate gravity lines, and the unbelievable breadth of the oscillation frequencies has never been produced by any electronic circuit that I know of!

Captain Johnson commented "you mentioned some time ago to me that you weren't really happy with the explanation given to the operation of Sonny, does this explain it now?"

James Whistler's eyebrows both raised up and he added, "It may well do but I would need to study both and compare results. The notion I have expressed would please those on mars because I have estimated the remaining life of this fireball based on what I have seen over the last few weeks or so, and it would be close to two hundred thousand years!

Now if we could drag this fireball to the Solar system, and position it somewhere near one of the moons that we are trying to exploit, it could give us the heat that we desperately need."

Eric Whistler opened his whiskey cabinet, "Hmmm, we are running a bit low on Space lubricant!"

The group enjoyed a sip as they all inwardly digested the latest information.

Henrik Svensson spoke "if you are right James, it would explain why other efforts to create a second Sonny have all failed so dismally. We were trying to initiate an atomic reaction when all the time it was something else entirely!"

Judder added "James, you are right, I can smell it! But your notion is more far reaching than even you have considered. Surely we will have to revise our ideas on what is going on in the sun and any other star for that matter."

"The Whistler gave one of his rare smiles, "let us not get too far ahead of ourselves here. What I am saying is a notion. That is all. A huge amount of controlled studying is now required. What is evident if I am right is that we cannot engineer these phenomena. They exist and that is all. If we can find one, we can possibly harness it, but I think they may be incredibly rare. We may have chanced upon one in our own system and one in the neighbouring system, and considering the vastness of that, the rarity could be likened to one molecule of water in the earths' seas. It really is that rare.

"We have to find a way to get this one back to the Solar system so that we can study it at the very least then," added Judder.

Eric Whistler realised the import of his mission and requested Captain Johnson to resume his lead role.

"Yes, very kind Eric!" said Captain Johnson ruefully accepting the offer. "Perhaps gentlemen we should all retire to our home vessels and consider what we may do to harvest this beast, reconvene here 08.00 hours in two days time, dismiss."

Eric asked Judder if he would stay on board the Space Adventurer because instinct told him that two heads being better than one, Judder and the Whistler would provide the best chance of a solution.

Captain Johnson nodded his approval and they all then retired to consider the possibilities

CHAPTER 35

The next assembly on the Space Adventurer was a quiet affair. All of the participants had fretted continuously about how to go about things, silence reigned.

Judder suddenly grinned and said "right this is how its gonna be!" the others smiled and waited for him to continue.

Judder suddenly became calm and using fingers of his hands made his seven points

- We cannot send this thing into the rethe on its own it would give a danger to any future jump attempted.
- It gives out an enormous amount of heat.
- If we go into the rethe with it we will have to have a big portal. I know that the cocoon will adjust itself to suit the size of intruding objects, but we would fry unless we do some thing about it.
- If we form a sort of guard around it and drag it up to as near warp factor one as we can get, await our arrival at a portal, then we could all make the jump as a composite group. We already know that a group can safely enter and exit the rethe.
- Once in the rethe we will not be in there for long and I suggest that we could all turn to point at it and hide behind our reflective laser shields that are still fitted after the mule saga. The Gravitas will need a shield to be added. It doesn't have one at the moment.
- We can use our diamond shards to orientate the entry angle so that we will come out on the extremes of the Solar system.

Due to previous experience I believe that although we will be pointing at, rather than away from the fireball due to a manoeuvre in the rethe, we will come out with our entry vector exactly. I do not have the mathematical skills to predict how long we will spend in the rethe but we could spend as much as temperature limits of our shield will permit and then turn away from the fireball and all give a synchronised blast on our rocket motors.

- Hey presto we are back in the Solar system, we finally drag the fireball to Gannymede or Europa or even Triton, establish its orbit and then get the hell outa there!

Judder sat down and waited for the laughter. It didn't come. Every other man there realised that Judder had covered the general points.

Judder walked to the Space lubricant cupboard and helped himself then turned and grinned. "Now you can get the experts onto that and they can get all the credit!"

Eric Whistler was taken aback by the shameless effrontery of Brian raiding his beloved drinks cabinet, but dammit he liked the man so much he had to keep moving his lips to hide the smile that was on them.

"Captain Johnson spoke out. "Now you know, Eric, what I had to put up with when you came on the scene!"

A good solid laugh went round the men and Captain Johnson said "well ok lets us see what is good and what is bad about his ideas."

A quick scan of the ships manifest found that Antonio Anthony was on the Gravitas so the designer of the shield was available. He was told of the revised purpose for the shield and to consider any improvements he could think of.

Antonio thought that in this case he did not want the reflected beam to focus any where, the exact opposite was needed. The heat rays reaching the ship had to be deflected and dispersed. In this instance he knew a liquid cooling may be necessary and reported back that it would take three weeks to modify the existing ones and add one to the Gravitas. He got on with that task.

Henrik Svensson presented them with the latest deep Space scan showing the location of the latest portals discovered. From this they selected one that would be at hand by the time they had accelerated the fireball up to the necessary speed.

Captain Johnson asked for a check on the number of Space suits available. Fortunately since Helen's venture with forced labour and the increased wealth of the Space administration organisation, earth had provided a proper suit for every individual on each ship, with a 5 percent contingency quantity. Captain Johnson decided that all crew members would wear a full Space suit during this jump, and that included the helmets, visors could be open until the jump was in progress.

The only thing not covered by Brian's little thesis was that the Space ships would drag the fireball to the correct point to enter the rethe but could not alter its course to be exactly as that of the Space ships.

The Whistler put on his thinking cap and began to construct a programme for his laptop after about four days he reported to Captain Johnson,

"We can not get the fireball to align itself exactly with the vector required by our diamond shards, but if we chose another portal than the one we selected the other day. It will be quite close, close enough any way so that it will not pull us substantially away from our destination. When we exit the rethe its course will diverge from ours and its speed is so high that we will only have a small time window to catch it up and using say Jupiter as our anchor, we can slow it down sufficiently to give us a choice of moons to aim for when deciding where we need it to orbit."

"Ok that sound like a goer," confirmed Captain Johnson "now where would be the best place to pen it up?"

The Whistler retired to his quarters to get some shut eye and then start his deliberations.

The following day the Whistler thought to himself, 'what about Titan. The place was cold but it did have forms of life. There was an active colony including the jail there. It could do with the heat, but it already had an atomic power station, and too much heat would or could cause flooding and disaster for the incumbents.

Europa also had its own atomic power station. This place may well develop life on its own but as we had found out with europan flu it could be dangerous. Earth was very cautious about Europa. So, back to Ganymede. There had been no signs of life or amino acid strings or anything else to suggest that life exist there. The Prof had postulated that an atomic power station was needed. The first one built had actually gone to Titan which had turned out to be a better choice.

Ganymede had nothing much to offer but it was fairly close to mars so comparative studies of the fireball and sonny would be relatively easy. It would be possible to establish an orbit that went round Jupiter and Ganymede, and the heat imparted by the fireball would be lost on the gas giant. The speed of the orbit would be such that it would only affect Ganymede for a couple of hours per orbit and so would not have an overwhelming effect on the place. Nevertheless if the heat was trapped inside lines of farm tents it could provide for some farming effort and was free. There would be no need for a nuclear power station. James Whistler considered other options such as orbiting it around mars, earth or Venus, but he could see major objections particularly from the non scientific world on earth and on mars. Venus would have been a waste of this valuable source of heat so Ganymede it was. Another advantage of choosing Ganymede was that if ever required it could be pulled out of the selected orbit and could be used to raise the temperature on mars so it would be very similar to that of earth.

He took his findings to the Captain for approval. The five way head to head was held to discuss his findings.

Judder was delighted to have scored good hits with his idea and could see the inescapable logic of the deviations proposed by the Whistler.

The mark two heat shield had been completed on the Gravitas and the upgrade was only two days away from completion on the other two ships.

The Whistler had the following to say about actions whilst in the rethe. He gave carefully calculated positional vectors to all three ship's captains but instructed only Captain Johnson on what to do. The other ships would take up their positions based on the position of the Solar Orbiter. There would be nothing much for Captain Johnson to do as the programme was a computor function, but initiating timing was of the utmost importance. The ships would be aligned along the travel axis of FB1 (fireball 1 would you believe!) and as a precaution all undercrew and non essential operations crew would move to the shadow side of each ship. The jump into the rethe would be made, Captain Johnson would start the relative position programme visually at the moment he was certain that the rethe had closed its cocoon. The ships would then automatically turn to point their heat shield at FB1. The heat rays reflected would be dispersed so as not to get back onto FB1. It was expected the heat rays would bounce back from the walls of the cocoon and gradually warm the entire ships structures, at this point they would have been in the rethe long enough to attempt an exit. Again Captain Johnson would initiate the second part of the automatic rethe programme and turn each ship if it needed it to be exactly at 120 degrees each with respect to the other. All ships computors being synchronised would give a good blast on the rocket motors and exit the rethe complete with their guest, then crews would resume normal stations.

The Whistler was proved once again to be expert. He got his calculations spot on. The return to the Solar system went absolutely according to plan. The major fear of not being able to control FB1 was unfounded it was put into an orbit round Jupiter and Ganymede. Someone coined the name 'bike chain orbit', and that pretty well described its shape. An announcement was made by Henrik Svensson over the intership broadcast system saying that the mission was concluded and the ships would go into geo stationary orbit around mars for some rest and recuperation. Of those anxious to get home the Freeloader was available and could be used as a taxi and if there were too many for the Freeloader, the Moneybag was expected to drop part of its cargo onto mars and would be able to take a fair few more. Any one wishing to stay aboard the mission ships could do so and those forming the skeleton crews would get triple pay for their efforts. Delighted crewmembers soon sorted themselves out and the shuttles began giving rides to the spacemen.

James Whistler was anxious to reacquaint himself with Ken Lee, and Ken offered the 'famous five' as some wag had christened them, a tour of the latest projects on mars.

Mars had expanded, there were now three big complexes and a number of smaller ones, cities and towns smiled Ken. The main complex was called Medusa. There were snake like avenues leading from the hub to the outer places which were known as Fingal's Caves. As the planet's water supply had improved more towns had sprung up some were still only village sized. An industrial region was in its embryo stages, and was called Marston. Similar attempts to name other villages met with derision due to the puerile efforts of some of the populace. No doubt suitable names would emerge but 'Old York' was booted out double quick. There were town councils but due to the smaller sizes of most grouped dwellings it was still easy to nip round to your councillor's house and let him know in person, just what you thought.

The shear volume of tree growth had to be seen to be believed, and the fish stocks were still being allowed to multiply with only limited fishing done.

Ken Lee knew the day was coming when he would have to permit the fishing enthusiasts their freedom to pursue their sport, but by then there would truly be ample stocks to support fishing in both commercial and leisure fields.

Mars now had dozens of species of flies and several more varieties of spiders.

There were herds of cows, sheep and goats, and a system of metalled roads was under construction.

Captain Johnson marvelled at the progress and congratulated Ken Lee on his progress. Ken on a more sober note admitted that the expansion rate was too big to last. He would have to slowly reduce the amount of money available and restore some control. "We will need more farms and farmers, so building will slow down but farming will increase. "I hope to strike a lucky balance just to keep everyone happy," he smiled, "James; I have heard a rumour that you have a better explanation about Sonny."

"Well it isn't classified information so you may as well know that I think I may well have. We have left what I think is a cousin of Sonny, orbiting Jupiter and Ganymede, and I propose to study them both closely before I go public. You know how disbelieving some characters are; you know when I fished your tooth out of that container, you should have seen the faces. The believers were delighted and the non believers were gob smacked. Real hard nosed reporters were convinced in a moment. Of course they all then wished to send us off on a mission impossible into the unknown, but I am a cautious man and I do nothing unless I have got well documented and accepted reasons for my action. And as any of our group will tell you it does not happen as simply as you may believe. We have unexplained time jumps to grapple with. There is plenty for us to do."

Captain Johnson joined with, "We have successfully established a colony on Stellar two which is a planet outside the solar system. We will have to visit them periodically. Their number is still less then two hundred but they have had children and they have to create an environment from even more basic conditions that you have here! This planet is an old one undergoing rejuvenation, but theirs is a new one just blossoming for the first time."

Ken Lee nodded, and asked if they had ever sampled Martian mushrooms. "These are not earth mushrooms but appear to be native to mars" he said "I had heard that fungi spores could survive many hundreds of years but these have survived many, many thousands of years. They seem to like to grow on the bark of our trees and prefer hardwood. They won't grow on pines!"

Kingdom Johnson smiled and said "I know a man who has successfully exported runner beans to Stellar two and I bet he would be delighted to try some of your mushrooms if they are non poisonous! When they re-boarded their ships for the final leg of the journey, Captain Johnson had a container with a gram or two of the Martian spores.

The inevitable party at the Prof's place followed.

CHAPTER 36

ANOTHER GOOD PARTY

As the folk arrived at the Prof's Brian and Nadine Judd were the last to arrive. The Prof welcomed them in. Judder had an expectant air about him, as he knew something was afoot and a voice commanded "turn round Brian."

Brian turned to see his mom Elizabeth standing in what can only be described as a wedding outfit, not the traditional white dress but an impeccably chosen ensemble. "Mom, when did this happen?" he asked.

"About two hours from now!" said the Prof.

Nadine was the only other person who had known about this in advance and said "did you get the priest I recommended?"

"She sure did" said a deep melodious voice from the other side of the room.

An imposing figure stood up and greeted every body as if he had known them all his life and asked, "well if we are all here we must proceed mustn't we?"

There was a hasty juggling for position as Brian Judd realised that he was in the unusual position of giving his mom away. Within the hour the marriage vows were done and dusted and the married couple sat down at the long edge of the table in the middle.

Nadine gave the couple her carefully concealed gift leaving the others with nothing to give, well almost nothing. Captain Johnson strode forward, gave the bride the customary kiss on the cheek and said "this will have to do for both of you, until we can get to the shops." He gave the Prof the container of Martian fungus.

"I told you we would have something unusual" marvelled the Prof, "that will keep me busy next spring."

"I think you should keep quiet about it I smuggled it past customs!" grinned Kingdom Johnson.

Jane Johnson murmured "well it is good to see that you weren't as tardy this time as last time cap!" it was three and a half years last time, so six weeks is a bonus to us."

The Whistler stood agape. He knew they were standing on the fringe of understanding something of time travel and a sudden truth dawned on him. It may be possible to compress or stretch time; in some way they had already done that, but travelling back or forward through time may not be anything other than a dream. Mind you he had thought that about travelling faster than the speed of light only a short while ago.

The priest standing to one side suddenly said "is this Catherine Whistler I see before me?" and he offered his hand. Catherine shook is hand and found her own hand lost inside the huge black fist. "I am the right reverend William Jackson, and I saw that TV interview. Did you know he is in jail now? I am from the dark end of our planet as was he. But my heart is light where his was consumed with some sort of hatred, I apologise on behalf of the rest of the human race."

Catherine said "well I don't think what he did to me was a jailable offence I only used those words to unsettle him!"

"Unsettle him, I think you destroyed him, but no one has lost any sleep over him. A number of people who had been on the wrong end of his interviews have put you forward for the Nobel peace prize, but I don't think you will get it!

As you know us black folk have been on the wrong end of injustice for far too long and it is good since the reformation that the playing field has been levelled. A serious mistake was made when well meaning liberals realising our plight tried to tilt the pitch in our favour to redress the balance. That was a bad mistake because you can not expect to cure racism with racism. I and a few others have fought to get the pitch exactly level, and now we just have to wait to see what goes on." Catherine was impressed with this gentle giant of a man and told him:-

"You will get a mention in my next book! It will be at the publishers shortly."

"Oh no, no, no, I wasn't trying to get publicity, its just that I so admired you for the way you handled that imbecile, that I, well I just had to speak to you."

"Well my second book is primarily to do with the era of faster than light travel, but all my characters got sucked into the Donkey's world and now into the reformation world and you are another notable piece in my tapestry. While I think of it you're not related to the right reverend Jesse Jackson are you?"

"I wish I was, but sadly no!"

"You *will* be in my book anyway. How did you get to be requested to perform this wedding?"

"Mrs. Judd there, our children go to the same school and well I flatter myself perhaps but I think she likes me!"

"I like you too so perhaps you aren't flattering your self!"

Catherine caught the Prof's eye and asked where all the kids were, she had complied with the request from Nadine to send hers to Nadine's house.

"They are all with Mrs. Jackson just now."

"Get them all here," said Catherine. Within the hour a shy Mrs. Jackson arrived with all of the Space Adventurer's kids and her own five children. She was made to feel doubly welcome, and the kids all rushed through into the back garden.

"There is another benefit of the reformation" Catherine informed the reverend, "children are allowed to be children. I absolutely hated it when those erstwhile liberal nincompoops thought that all children should be given sex education right from when they are tiny. Childhood, is the age of innocence, and should be guarded at all costs."

William Jackson beamed at her. "If I had anything to do with it you would get that Nobel prize!"

"I can assure you that every woman here believes that, except well I don't know about Mrs. Jackson"

"Hannah" he boomed, "Tell what you think about childhood to Catherine here!"

Hannah spoke almost what Catherine had just said not word for word, but certainly sentiment for sentiment.

Catherine said "good on yer Hannah, we can fix it together!" Hannah visibly relaxed and the reverend moved away talking and smiling as he went.

Catherine said out loud "ok girls about now I should think!"

"What a swell party this is!" they chorused. Hannah split her sides laughing.

Catherine knew she had made another good friend and hoped the others would like Hannah equally. The Prof and his new bride circulated amongst the guests, and retired early. After all they were getting on a bit. Oh yes? Old age was the furthest thing from their minds as they retired for the night. The party went on until the early hours and children were found snoozing in some peculiar places. They slept where they fell and rather than disturb them Hannah Jackson found a number of blankets and draped them over the recumbent forms. The following day was a Saturday and the kids were all up and about early demanding to be fed. The moms were up next. By the time the men trooped down breakfast was over so they had to feed themselves. The Prof and Liz as she liked to be known had still barely scratched the surface as each tried to fill the other with details from their previous life.

"I have definitely retired from the Space service now, so I'm glad Brian is continuing the family tradition. When I look back now, he cropped up under the name of Keith Windridge, but even then I somehow liked him and at the very early times even before these parties, I noticed that he had a little scar behind his one ear. Well I am perceptive enough to have made the full conclusion from that alone. I didn't dare think it though in case it wasn't true!"

Liz spoke with a choked voice, "People said over the years that he was very like me, and I had the idea right deep inside me that perhaps I wasn't just a stranger. But I have seen adopted children grow up and they begin to resemble their adoptive parents, so I didn't dare hope!"

"We have both lost a dear partner and we are neither of us dead yet!" she gave him a guilty glance as he then continued "We have only one life and most folk only get one chance. We have got a second chance and we are going to enjoy it. Objections, Mrs Wild?"

"None at all, Mr. Wild!"

CHAPTER 37

ANOTHER STUDY OF SONNY

Doctor Barry captained the next mission which was to study sonny and FB1.

After protracted observations during which time the Whistler made copious notes, he concluded that the last explanation of Sonny was quite close. The only thing different was that the core reaction was not nuclear but ether-rethe oscillatory. Only the central core had this link to the rethe and was balanced exactly. The amount of matter on the outer extremities was almost immaterial but it served to store the heat. The temperature in the heart of each of these fireballs was extraordinarily high and did allow a limited nuclear fusion reaction, just outside the central cocoon. This reaction would almost certainly stop if for any reason the central core ceased to oscillate. So now we had a calculable amount of radiation and a means to estimate the life of the reaction, the Whistler knew that readings taken fifty years apart would provide a much more accurate basis for his conjecture but he believed from his revised calculations that the reaction inside Sonny would go on for about two hundred thousand years and FB1 could last some twenty five percent longer. I do not have the scientific knowledge to go further into the explanation, but I have confidence in the Whistler and so I merely report his opinion as fact.

Note from Catherine Whistler: the faster than light era is well and truly upon us now but it seems to me that we are on the verge of at least partial time travel so at this point I think that book two is complete. I shall send the

King of England a copy because without his help I may never have been able to publish.

An original story by DAVID DONALD KEIRLE. November 2009. The author acknowledges that his ideas have been influenced by things that he has read over the years and thanks all who have gone before.

ABOUT THE AUTHOR

The author was born in 1940, during the dark days of the war. Nevertheless, he enjoyed a good childhood and a reasonable education, culminating in grammar school and, finally, technical college, where he studied as an electrical engineer, travelling the world as part of his duties.

Retiring in 2005, he decided to see if he had a book in him, the results of which are now laid before you in the form of a trilogy.